**This special signed edition
is limited to 500 numbered copies
and 26 lettered copies.**

This is copy _____.

AZTECHS

AZTECHS

Lucius Shepard

Subterranean Press · 2003

FIRST EDITION

ISBN
1-931081-50-6

Subterranean Press
P.O. Box 190106
Burton, MI 48519

email:
publisher@subterraneanpress.com

website:
www.subterraneanpress.com

PART ONE

Papa's always saying there's too many people in the world, but what's he know...Old fool! Sitting home alone all day with his mezcal and his reefer. Drifting, dozing, dreaming. He never sees anyone, don't talk to no one except me. Nobody real that is. He talks to Mama's ghost, to the way she was back when she was fine and twenty-nine. I got the house fixed up nice, but he never lets me touch his room. Walls covered with brown butcher paper to hide holes in the plaster, and a photograph of him and Mama tacked up to cover a tear in the paper—looks like a stamp on a package, like this parcel he was carrying exploded in around him, got inverted somehow so the postage wound up on the inside, and he just sits there in the middle of it, getting mailed off to nowhere.

I was in the bathroom the other night, checking out the hair, the jacket, when he yells, "Eddie!" I cracked the door, peered down the hall and saw him at his table, goofing on the photograph. He's a youthful forty in the picture, hair gathered into a ponytail under a funky straw hat, wearing a T-shirt with the word REVOLUTION printed on it and beneath that the slogan, You Are What You Rebel Against. He's got an arm around Mama, who's shading her eyes against the sun, and there I am too, because you see it's a breezy day, and the summer dress she's got on is molded to the ripening curve of her belly, evidence that Eddie Poe is on his way to the world. They're on the San Diego side, about to cross over and lead a demonstration against Sony Corporation for exploiting the Mexican worker, but it looks as if they're heading off to fuck on the beach at Hermosillo.

"Eddie...Goddammit!"

"Hang on a minute!" I said. "Okay?"

I figured out years ago why Papa loves that picture. It shows the last time they were happy. That night they were visited by some government types who played them a video featuring some of Papa's less notorious co-conspirators getting their throats cut.

"Want to be with the beaners?" one guy asked Papa. "You got our permission. Go be with 'em. But you come back to the States, we'll kill your ass. Try any legal bullshit, we'll kill you for that. It'll make a stink for a while, a loudmouth like you talking through his neck. All your movie star pals, they'll be outraged. But it'll blow over. Know why? In the grand scheme of things, your cause is shit!"

Papa called everyone he could think of who might help, but nobody could guarantee our safety, and when more of his friends turned up dead, he realized no amount of publicity could immunize us against the retribution of the various corporate entities who were determined to stabilize the profit environment they had established on the border. Mama died during a flu epidemic a couple of years afterward, and Papa's health was broken by nearly two decades of working in the Sony *maquiladora*. I liked to think if I'd been in his position, with a young wife and a baby on the way, I'd have bailed on my principles to keep them safe—but it was a hard sell.

"Where you going tonight, Eddie?" he said as I swung on into his room. Before I could answer, he came back with, "Out to crawl in the sewer with the rest of the insects, I suppose." He juiced his voice with an extra hit of disdain. "Watching you waste your life makes me sick at heart. The way you're going, son, you've got no future."

I was twenty-four years old and ran my own security service. Considering I'd grown up a *gringo puro* in one of the toughest barrios in Mexico, an illegal alien, a wetback in reverse, I'd done all right for myself. But Papa didn't see it that way—he held me to a standard he couldn't meet himself.

"I got no future?" I said, stepping close. "Who the fuck's fault you figure that is?"

He refused to acknowledge me, his grizzled face like a clenched fist, eyes locked on the photograph of him and Mama.

"I wish I had the fuckin' time to sit around and cultivate my mind," I said. "Who knows what I might achieve? I might get to be a college professor with his head so far up his ass, he got nothin' better to do than poke his nose places it ain't wanted."

"You never..." he began, but I talked right through him.

"And if I developed a *really* big brain, I might be able to screw things up so bad, I'd wind up livin' in shit the rest of my life."

"Just because you've become inured to the way things are," he said, "that doesn't mean I was wrong to want to change them."

"Right...I forgot. You the revolutionary. A real leftist hero. Well, I don't see you fuckin' mannin' the barricades now. All you do is sit and stare at that stupid picture! Here!" I dug into my jacket pocket, fingered out a plastic packet containing a dozen blue gelatin caps, and tossed them onto the table. "Wanna trip on your picture? These'll put you right in there."

He glanced at the pills but didn't touch them.

"Go on...take 'em! I got 'em special for you." I was so messed up behind the argument, my emotions were confused, and though I was enraged, I felt like crying and putting my arms around him.

He prodded the packet with a forefinger. I knew he was dying to take them, and this too was a cause of emotional confusion—I intended the pills to make him happy, but I also took pleasure in his weakness. He slit the seam of the packet, let the capsules dribble out onto the table, then said in a subdued tone, "What're you doing tonight, son?"

"I'm gonna meet Guadalupe at Cruzados. We got business."

He made a scornful noise.

"What's wrong with you, man?" I said. "Lupe's more honey than god. She's my pale Spanish girl."

He held a gelatin capsule up to the light—a gem dealer checking the water of a sapphire. "The woman's playing you," he said.

"Everyone plays everyone else. It's the Master's plan."

"Yes, but she's much better at it than you."

I started getting angry again. "I gotta go," I told him.

"How many of these do I take?" He had a handful of the pills.

"How fucked up you wanna get?"

His eyes cut toward the photograph. "Extremely," he said.

●

Papa and I lived in what once was known as Mexicali, but had become an almost indistinguishable part of a single city that stretched from the Gulf to the Pacific, cozied up like a snake against the 1200-mile-long laser fence designed to wall off America from the poor, the tired, the hungry, the oppressed masses yearning for freedom. The fence—like the city it damned—had come to be called El Rayo, and living next to that enormous bug zapper, that fiery curtain hung between 100-foot-high titanium poles...well, they used to say living under power lines caused cancer, but living next to El Rayo caused cancer of the mind, the soul. It's not what it was intended to be that made it so devastating, though a sheet of fire that could charbroil your ass however fast you passed through it was certainly the latest thing in barriers, the ultimate statement of contempt and disinterest. No, it's like Papa once said, something that big is more magical than actual, more destructive as a symbol than as an isolationist tactic. When they switched it on, midnights along the border became red forever after, and everything that happened from that day forth took on that bloody color. Every action, every emotion, every dream.

First thing I noticed as I stepped out the door was El Rayo, like a blood-red wave about to break over us, standing seventy feet above the rooftops, its glare staining the starless reach of the sky, making that zoned-out humming sound. Then the rest of the street snapped into focus, a single-file herd of lowriders humping and fucking the pavement, giant metal roaches tattooed with hellfire, images of the Virgin, slogans. Demented bearded faces inside, arms and legs poking out the windows. Those things never go out of style, that grinding *racha chacha chacha* sound they make, speakers blasting out salsa, border reggae, warped *conjuntos*, Malaysian pop, music from a million places jammed together into one big scratchy, bumping, throbbing noise that put grooves on the inside of your skull. They rocked along in a jangle of light past appliance shops with Aztec temples painted on their facades, bodegas, clubs, souvenir shops, their bright windows aglitter with crystal crosses gilt madonnas rhinestone eagle knives flashing in miles of red midnight, little stucco caves with corrugated iron doors rolled partway down, interiors littered with every form of cheapness: mirrors with ornate tin frames, torrero capes with airbrushed scenes from the Plaza del Toros, sombreros festooned with embroidery and bits of broken mirror, switchblades with dragons worked in gold paint you could scrape off with your thumbnail. Watching from the curb were whores stuffed into dresses that looked like napkinholders cinched around globs of brown fat, their faces like images painted on a sideshow facade, rouge-dappled cheeks and starred eyes and oohing crimson mouths opening onto funhouse rides. Cruel, dark male faces stared from the doorways and alley mouths. Carved eyebrows and lava flows of black hair, eyes black magnets and gold-glinting teeth, mustaches sharply drawn as scythes, neon-lit coils of cigarette smoke slithering from their lips. Vendors pushing fruit drinks, *bocadillos*, ices, shish kebabs of dead dog slathered with red sauce, knock-offs of high-tech toys...I used to have this dream about El Rayo, I'd come swooping down in a plane, cutting so low my wingtip would brush the fire, then I'd climb way high so I could see the entire length of it and wonder if the men who built it recognized the sinister shape they had called into being. What immense signal were they flashing out into nowhere? What character did it form? What meanings did it have in how many alphabets? With what secret societies and cosmic institutions did it align? Seeing it that way. I understood that nothing in this world existed for the reasons stated by Einstein, and that nothing Einstein ever said made any sense except on the level of pure magic, because at the bottom of all that mathematical boogaloo is just jungle noise and street rhythms and a vast primitive design.

Cruzados constituted something of an irony as related to El Rayo in that you could enter the club from either side of the border. The laser fence cut through the center of the place, obscured behind roll-down metal doors. The management had rigged subterranean charges that would jolt the transmitters every hour on the hour, causing a three-second interval in the beam, and during that interval you could jump across from Mexico to the States or vice versa. It may seem strange that this was permitted, but illegal crossings on a small scale weren't considered a problem—both sides of the border, after all, shared the same economy, the same terrible pollution and crime rate, and La Migra kept watch on the American side to make certain that no one truly dangerous, like Papa, slipped into the Land of the Free.

I loved the darkness of the club, the little orange candleflames in glass cups on all the tables, the iron door that hourly would slide up to reveal El Rayo, the lion heartbeat rhythm of the background music, the curving black and chrome bar. It was my office, my soul's true home. I grabbed a seat at the bar, and the bartender seemed to glide on a track toward me, his silver teeth cutting a crescent smile, eyes gleaming black bugs, sideburns pointy black stillettos...

"Can I bring you something, Mister Poe?"

"Orlando! *Buenas noches,*" I said. "Tequila and a beer back."

The television above the bar was playing El Rayo's Greatest Hits. Showing how people tried to cross in the early years after the barrier was switched on, at the moment focusing on one guy who had covered his car with cheap mirrors, because he'd heard mirrors reflect lasers, but had not known the mirrors needed to be perfect, and drove straight into the barrier, emerging on the other side as a smoking wad of melted glass and steel. The tape contained dozens of such idiot plays. There was another tape of people making pilgrimages to the barrier, building altars and shrines beside it, and sometimes throwing themselves into the fire; but that one wasn't as popular, because people still did that shit.

Orlando brought my tequila and beer, and I asked him what was up. He relaxed somewhat from his pose of evil suavity and said, "You know that *chingado* Tonio Fernandez? Got that TV show in San Diego talks about border issues...all that shit? Yeah, well he hears how Guty Cardenas...Remember him? Junior welter champ 'bout eight, nine years ago? Okay. So Tonio hears how he's all fucked up on drugs. Guty dopes at my uncle's place in TJ. I see him there all the time. And Tonio decides he's gon' come down and lay this Mexican Jesus soul trip on him...get him clean, right." Orlando paused to light a cigarette and blew a silvery glowing ring. "This is funny, because Tonio's 'bout as Mexican as a goddamn bag of Cheetos. The guy talks like a fuckin' Baptist. Guty couldn't get away from his ass fast enough. I mean, even dope hell's better'n that shit, you know. He does not want to be saved. Does not want to be resurrected or rocked out of his depression. He wants to go down the hole with a grin on his fuckin' face. He refuses to be turned into a splendid clean splinter of what he once was and paraded out as a rehab wonder. Like, see what can be made of these raw materials with the proper Christian conditioning..."

My message center buzzed. I told Orlando I'd catch the rest of his story later and touched a button on the counter. A screen and a keypad popped up from the bar; I punched in a code. Seconds later, a muscular guy in a wifebeater undershirt was staring back at me from the screen. His trapezius bulked up from his shoulders like foothills flanking the mountain of his head. His face, shadowed by a few days' growth of beard, was the hard, contemptuous face of somebody who liked to hurt people. I'd never seen him before, didn't know his name, but I could tell he was Sammy by the unblinking eyes and reflexive clump of his jaw muscles, by his precision of speech and utter lack of inflection and the sergeant's stripes tattooed on his cheek. Since the beginning of the Pan-Mayan War, vets addicted to the samurai drug had been settling this side of the border where no one would try to outlaw their violent subculture. They had proved a significant asset to the economy; their no-holds-barred pit fights were a major tourist attraction and they provided a terrific source of expert muscle for people like me. The ex-sergeant had a flesh-colored adhesive patch affixed to his neck that released a steady supply of his favorite poison into his system. That struck me as odd. Most of his kind preferred an implant—implants were harder to rip off during a fight.

"Eddie Poe?" the ex-sergeant said.

I switched his voice to my earphone and said, "Talk fast."

All the muscles of his face appeared to ripple—he didn't like my tone, I guess. "Larry Crespo is dead," he said after regaining control.

That was bad news, but I didn't trust the source. "How'd you get this number?"

"From Crespo. He thought you might be able to use me."

"What a coincidence. Here I am short one Crespo, and you just happen to call."

Considering my disrespect, I figured he would have loved to tear me apart; but his control was excellent. People not of the tribe pissed Sammy off under the best of circumstances.

The buzzcut guy spoke through his teeth. "If you're insinuating I killed him...Crespo was part of my seven."

I wasn't that familiar with Sammy culture, but I knew that "my seven" referred to a blood bond. By telling me this, he was declaring his innocence in a persuasive fashion. But I was still suspicious—I didn't like accidents, especially on an important job.

"What's your name, Sarge?" I asked.

"Lawton Childers."

"Got a resume?"

"You should already have it."

"Oh, yeah." I tapped a key and the resume appeared on-screen. "I see you worked for the Carbonells recently. Got any problem with killin' a few of 'em?"

"Be my pleasure," said Childers without expression.

"Probably won't be necessary." I studied the remainder of the resume. "I need quality work tonight. Restraint is key. You'll be protectin' a representative of AZTECHS during a negotiation with the Carbonells."

"Understood," Childers said.

"What's your impression of the Carbonells?"

Childers' smile developed slowly—an emblem of ferocity. "They're not half as bad as they think they are."

"That's not what I'm askin'," I told him. "You have any insights into their personalities might be helpful?"

"I paid no attention to their personalities." Childers said.

I continued reading the resume. "Three tours in Guatemala. Damn, you musta loved your country!" I gave him a sardonic wink.

Childers stood mute.

"You haven't done much bodyguard work," I said. "Why now?"

"I'm going to need the operation."

In Sammy parlance, "the operation" was a bioengineering procedure to overcome a decline in sensitivity to the drug.

"How's your tolerance now?" I asked.

"I killed an ape in a pit fight last weekend. You can verify it."

"Somebody's pet monkey? King Kong? What?

"Orangutan."

I didn't like switching horses in midstream, but since my horse was dead, I had little choice, and if the drugs had boosted Childers's combat abilities to the point where he had taken out an orangutan in hand-to-hand, he might be a better bargain than Crespo. "All right," I said. "The recording of this transmission will be our contract. I'm hirin' you for the duration of the job. Standard terms. Bonus to be determined."

Childers only reaction was to nod.

"The men you'll be workin' with...Crespo's team. Any problems there?"

"None."

"Okay. See you later tonight."

"Don't you want to know how Crespo died?"

Sammy usually displayed an indifferent attitude to life and death, so this question seemed against type. Childer's expression had barely changed during our brief interview, but now I could have sworn I detected a glimmer of outrage at my indifference. "I assumed it was the drugs," I told him.

"His neck was broken." Childers scratched the tiny chevrons on his cheek with a forefinger as big as a corn dog. "Nice and neat."

Sammy killing Sammy was how I figured it, because the only person capable of kevorking a drugged mesomorphic maniac like Crespo would be another drugged mesomorphic maniac. But Sammy killing Sammy outside the pit wasn't that common, and Crespo had been a renowned pitfighter, an icon to his brothers-in-dope. "Any ideas who?" I asked.

Childers shook his head with the ponderous slowness of a statue just coming to life. "Some dangerous motherfucker."

"As dangerous as you?"

"You never know."

"See you tonight," I said, and cleared the screen.

PART TWO

I sucked on the tequila, considering the possibility of hiring another Sammy or two, but I decided that more muscle might stir up the Carbonells. I checked my watch. Seven-twenty-two. Nearly Guadalupe time. I fumbled in my jacket pocket, dug out a blue gelatin capsule I'd held back from Papa and swallowed it with a sip of beer. As I waited for the blue to take effect, I gave thought to what Papa had said about Guadalupe. I'd never doubted that she was using me to further her career. In the land of a million channels, she was a rising star, and through me, she had access to stories with which she fleshed out her weekly show, two hours of border news interspersed with sex, much of it featuring yours truly and Srta. Guadalupe Bernal. I had hopes that our relationship might evolve past the level of a business association, and it was this that caused Papa to believe I was being chumped. But in my limited appreciation of life, chumped or not, I was almost completely fulfilled to be the owner of a security service and the semi-famous saddle pard of the Border Rose.

By eight o'clock I was surfing a bright blue wave of psychotropic love sweet love, and my natural horniness had been elevated to the level of moonstruck monkey. At eight sharp the metal door at the center of the club rattled upward, and the heated glow of El Rayo filled in all the shadows, casting red gleams along the countertop and blazing in the mirror. Then a little seismic shudder, the curtain of fire vanished, and Lupe came striding into the Mexican side of the club, her camera scooting along at her heels, a steel six-legged cross between a lizard and a bug about the size of a chihauhua, the technology courtesy of AZTECHS. The fire returned, framing her like Our Lady of Guadalupe as she came toward me. Tall and slender and pale, she had on white slacks and a silky red open-collared blouse embroidered with black roses. The door rattled down, returning Cruzados to its customary dimness—she appeared to glow against the backdrop.

She settled on the stool next to mine, the coils of her perfume slithering around me, and gave me a quick wet kiss. Her face was made up for the show. Shellacked crimson lips and eyes transformed into dark butterfly wings with brushed-on shadow; but I could see down to the Iberian geometry of broad cheekbones and narrow chin and strong nose. She leaned into me and whispered, "Can we get private, baby? I need a new tape to intercut with the opening."

We walked along a corridor that angled off from the main room and found an unoccupied roomette.

Black walls, black couch with chrome trim, offset lighting. The Marquis de Sade would have been happy there. We undressed hurriedly and made love while the camera skittered about the walls above us, beside us, poised like a praying mantis, beaming jewels of light onto our skin. Usually Lupe liked me to talk shit to her, give her a slow, coarsely self-referential fuck, but tonight's show would likely be picked up by other shows, and so we kept it classy, just sighs and whispers as we went heartbeat-to-heartbeat from the center of the carnal border nighttime trance life, borderless between people, between nations, part of the radio holeo video feelio fuckio stream of images dancing along that red snakebelly line that linked ocean to ocean. I was stained all the way through with Lupe. Her breath was my breath, and we were swimming upstream in the red midnight, offering our all to the vast cable syndrome. I felt those images coursing along my skin, like a hundred thousand cats-per-second rubbing against me, and afterward, lying quietly while Lupe restored her makeup, perched on the edge of the couch beside me, I could still feel them moving ghostlike around us.

"Frankie," she said, and the camera-bug-lizard turned its snoutlike lens housing toward her. "Play the opening."

A holographic shot of Lupe in her white slacks and red blouse appeared in the center of the room against a background of sage, sand, and cactus, and her diminished voice began to speak:

Twenty-three years ago somebody erected a sign in the desert. Out in the middle of nowhere, 150, 160 miles due east from Hermosillo on the Pacific coast. Just a plain wooden sign, billboard-sized, bearing three words neatly lettered in black paint:

REALITY STOPS HERE

"Start intercutting the sex here," Lupe told Frankie. "Alternate between me'n Eddie and shots of me on the desert."

There was no apparent reason for a sign—it marked no road, no building, no watercourse, no natural formation of any significance. The place where it stood was at the heart of a trackless waste of cactus and sand and scorpions. The first person known to have seen it was a snake hunter in a jeep who claimed to have shot it full of holes, but when someone checked it out a few days later, they found it undamaged. That story seemed to piss people off, or at the least to offer an irresistible challenge; they took to vandalizing the sign on a regular basis, driving in from Hermosillo, from the border, and eventually from places as far away as Monterrey and San Luis Potosi. After each incident the sign would reappear good as new, sometimes within a few hours of being burned or chainsawed or shotgunned, with no evidence left to indicate who had done the repairs.

"Now I want to hear the heavy breathing," Lupe said; she glanced at me and smiled. "Nice moves, Eddie. You take somethin' tonight?"

"Just a blue," I said.

"Oh." She gave me a poochy look. "You must love me a lot, huh?"

"Don't break the mood," I told her. "I'm happy."

The consensus came to be that the sign must be some sort of hoax—the phrase REALITY STOPS HERE *had the ring of art school bullshit. However, this viewpoint absorbed a major hit when a scientist from the university in Mexico City, made curious by reports of the sign's magical invulnerability, dynamited it and, along with a handful of assistants and a battery of cameras, staked out the area. Twelve hours later the sign was back. Though they swore they hadn't fallen asleep, neither the scientist nor his assistants could recall how this had happened; nor was the film they shot of much help. The cameras had recorded eleven hours fifty-nine minutes and fifty-four seconds of the wreckage lying undisturbed; this was followed by a static-filled gap of six seconds duration. When the static ceased, the sign was as before, and the wreckage had vanished.*

"Okay," said Lupe. "Start strobing the sex."

Thereafter the area for miles around the sign came to be thought of as a kind of desert Bermuda Triangle. Disappearances and apparitions were reported, supernatural legends were spawned. Except for crazies and the odd researcher, people stayed clear of the region. Then, ten years after the sign had first been sighted, it vanished. However, the spot where it had stood did not remain vacant for long. It was replaced several days later by a stone head some three and a half stories tall, rendered in the style of the Aztecs and representing the emperor overthrown centuries before by the conquistadors, Montezuma. Lying on its side, pitted and crumbling, it looked from a distance to be the relic of a dead culture; but when seen close at hand, it became clear that this was not a fragment of an ancient statue, but the logo of some thoroughly modern organization.

AZTECHS.

A shot of the great stone head replaced Lupe's face. Its eyes were television screens, and across them drifted fleeting images of the natural world. Birds in flight, coyotes skulking, a serpent unwinding across hardpan, elephants fording a river...

"Let's drop the image of the sex into the head's eye screens." said Lupe. "Then close in on one of the screens during the next section." She glanced at me over her shoulder. "Nice, huh?"

"Very," I said.

When the AZTECHS *shops began to appear all along the border, selling revolutionary technology at cut-rate prices, using the stone head as their logo, the mystery seemed to be solved. But one part of the mystery remained unrevealed....*

Lupe began to relate the story of how an American military AI, who had since taken to calling itself Montezuma, had succeeded in downloading a copy of itself into a Mexican storage unit, wiping out its original, and establishing a virtual kingdom in the deep desert, guaranteeing its survival by means of contracts between its then-secret business entity, the AZTECHS Corporation, and multinational conglomerates all over the world—contracts that, if breached, would have catastrophic results for the global economy. As Frankie caused the holographic image to shift into increasingly tighter displays of the stone head, its broad face and thick-lipped mouth seeming to express a mournful calm, I watched Lupe and me getting nasty in the left eye screen. I had a few insecurities about the relationship. We had a powerful physical attraction for one another, but sex was a currency between us. Like Papa said, Lupe was playing me, and I was playing her, using my celebrity to create new business opportunities. Despite knowing all this was true, despite being okay with it, I was still upset by what he had said, and I tried to find some sign in our performance that Lupe and I were about more than business, that hidden in the squirming imagery flickering across the eye screen were the telltales of a deeper attraction—not because I hoped for this so much (so I told myself), but simply because I wanted to prove Papa wrong.

"When you do the fade," Lupe said to Frankie, "pull it back and let 'em hear me come."

The image of the stone head dwindled to the tune of Lupe's moans and outcries. She stood and gazed at me with an expression of exaggerated concern. "What's the matter, Eddie? You look sad."

"Nothin'." I started buttoning my shirt. "Just Papa's on my ass again."

"You should move outa there," Lupe said, running a hand along my shoulder.

"Yeah, maybe." I sat up.

"What'd he say to you?"

I filled her in.

"*You* got no future?" Lupe sniffed in disdain. "That old fuck should talk!"

"He said you were playin' me," I said.

"Playin' *with* you, maybe."

"Whatever." I got to my feet, pulled on my slacks. Lupe picked up my shoulder harness. "New gun?"

"New to me. I bought it off Sammy. I figure it did some damage down in Guatemala." She toyed with the settings on the handle of the weapon, and I snatched it from her. "Don't mess with it," I told her. "You'll blow somethin' up. Way you got it set, it fires grenades."

"Ooh, nice!" She petted the gun and gave me a flirty smile. "I feel so safe with you."

This teasing bullshit was normal Lupe mode, and I was used to it; but it irritated me then. "Do you?" I said.

She looked at me, puzzled. "Huh?"

"All this jokin' around we do," I said, "I wanna know if you really mean it. You feel safe with me?"

She turned her back, folded her arms. "I don't need this!"

"Yeah? Well, I wanna know what's goin' on." I turned her to face me. "Y'know, sometimes when we're fuckin', I can feel you. Right with me, right where I am in my head. I know it's true. But I'd like to hear it from you."

She stood mute, refusing to meet my eyes.

"C'mon!" I said. "Let's clear this up. You don't care nothin' 'bout me, lemme hear it."

"What I feel," she said angrily, "ain't got nothin' to do with this. I told you a thousand times, I'm alla 'bout career. You wanna know if I *love* you?" She gave "love" a sneering emphasis.

"Do you?"

She glanced up at me, and I could have sworn I detected a softening of her hard shell, but only for an instant. "If I do or if I don't, what's it matter? This is business, Eddie. I ain't gon' let emotion fuck it up."

Frankie was pointing his lens at me, clinging to the wall a few feet away. I took a swipe at him, and he spider-walked away. "Are you shootin' this?" I asked Lupe. "You shootin' this right now?"

"Read your contract. I can shoot any thing I want 'long as we're together."

"Screw you!" I shrugged into the harness and scooped up my jacket. "Let's go."

"But we'll be early! I thought we could have a drink."

"We get there early, Frankie can take some nude shots of you with the head." I'd intended this as sarcasm, but I could tell Lupe thought it was a terrific idea.

LUCIUS SHEPARD

Week Two

The man we had been hired to protect that night, the official spokesman for the AZTECHS Corporation, billed himself as Z2 (as in Montezuma 2). His face was identical to that of the stone head, and speculation held that he'd had some work done, that the AI had gotten hold of some poor bastard lost in the desert and given him a new face, new everything. Whoever he had been, he was a superstar now, and I broke out the limo for him, an old refurbished black Rolls with so much armor, Godzilla couldn't have dented it with a hammer.

We drove south into the desert and after slightly more than an hour came in sight of the head. With its glowing eyes and partially eroded features and massive stoic gloom, it had a bewitched air, as if it were in some terrible way alive, condemned to inhabit this wasteland of sage and scorpions and organ-pipe cactus, to stare blindly into forever, displaying but not seeing the images of the things it once had loved. Lupe went off to pose beside the head, and I dialed back the roof of the limo and sat gazing at the stars. They were so bright, the desert sand looked blue in their light, and the low sage-covered hills stood out in sharp relief against the sky. I wasn't nervous, but I was working on nervous, imagining everything that could go wrong when you were dealing with vicious bastards like the Carbonells. The old cartels had been seriously violent, but the Carbonells, along with the Guzman family, and the recently united youth gangs, who went by the name Los de Abajo...they had taken viciousness to a new level. Mass murder, in their view, should be certified as an Olympic sport. I'd been surprised when the Carbonells had agreed to let Lupe shoot the negotiation, but now I recognized that exposing their criminal activities on a show with an international viewing audience was a validation of their power. They didn't care who knew what they were doing. Try and stop us was their attitude. We're a law unto ourselves.

Sammy, who had followed the Rolls in an armored personnel carrier, established a perimeter and stood watch, stubby AR-20s at the ready, all four men wearing desert camo and plastic armor, carrying light packs. I'd worked with Crespo's team before. Fetisov had pale blond hair, a Russian icon tattooed on his back. Dennard, like Crespo, was a big time pitfighter, an Afro-American with Egyptian hieroglyphs tattooed on his lips and eyelids. Morely had been a sniper and there were dozens of tiny blue humanoid shapes tattooed on his chest, the record of his kills in Honduras and Guatemala. I hadn't yet seen Childers' body art, but I supposed it would be a self-advertisement similar to Moreley's, a few dozen souls rendered into exclamation points or black roses. But they all sported the basic Sammy look—buzzcut, staring, heavily muscled, grim. Months before, I'd visited Crespo at his home, the Green Rat Compound. High stone walls topped with all manner of security devices, enclosing an old hotel, three stories of green stucco and a dusty courtyard where fighters trained day and night. It was a weird combination of prison, barracks, dojo, and monastery. Sammy hated music—any kind of music drove him up the walls—and so the only thing you heard were enraged shouts from the courtyard and chanted strength mantras. Bulked-up men of every description sat in solitary cells and refined their drugged focus; others lifted weights and toughened their limbs by striking a variety of rigid objects. Walking through the place, I felt like a baby deer in a lion cage. I guess it would be accurate to say that Sammy addicts were the rodeo clowns of the junkie universe, the baddest, most functional and most trustworthy of their kind.

At twenty to one, Dennard gave the alert. I climbed out of the limo and looked to where he was pointing. Off to the left of the head, some forty yards away, was a rise sentried by organ-pipe cactus. A rider on horseback appeared to be watching us from atop it, and soon he was joined by two more riders. Their silhouettes black as absences against the stars. Something about the way they moved astride their mounts tweaked my neck hairs. They remained on the crest for a minute or so, then wheeled their horses and rode out of sight. Shortly thereafter, Z2, wearing a pale gray suit and matching shirt, came walking toward us from behind the rise, walking with a confident step. He passed Sammy by without acknowledgment and addressed himself to Lupe, who—flushed and excited—had run over to stand beside me. "Senorita Bernal," he said. *"Encantada."*

He turned to me and said, "I trust there have been no changes, Senor Poe."

"None," I told him. "We'll have you at Ramiro's house by three, After that…" I shrugged. "Who can say?"

"No one but God," he said, and smiled. "But God is watching us tonight. You can be sure of that."

As we drove toward El Rayo, Z2 sat in a backwards-facing seat, Lupe beside him, with Frankie clinging upside-down to the roof, shooting the interview, such as it was. The spokesman answered every question with polite demurrals and a Jesus-loves-you smile. Whereas the stone head projected a feeling of gloom, its human twin had about him an aura of unflappable serenity. It was a nice way to be—for him, anyway—but I doubted that Ramiro Carbonell would be impressed. Z2's answers grew increasingly nonresponsive. My anxieties had kicked in, and his beatific evasion was beginning to piss me off.

"Hey," I said, interrupting Lupe mid-question and addressing the spokesman. "What do people call you, man? Like when you're havin' a drink with friends, they go, 'Pass the beer nuts, Zee Two?' Or you gotta nickname?"

Frankie whirred, likely adjusting his lens to include me in the shot.

"Zee," the spokesman said, unperturbed. "You may call me Zee."

"Zee. Okay. So what's your story, Zee? Who were you 'fore you landed this gig?"

"I am who I am," he said.

"Oh...sure. That clears things up. 'Cause, see, I was thinkin' you were *not* who you were."

Zee's smile was an emblem of infinite patience. "Would you ask a gourd filled with new wine how it was to be filled with dirty water?"

"I wouldn't ask a gourd shit," I said. "That'd be stupid."

Zee spread his hands as if to say I had made his point.

"But you ain't no fuckin' gourd," I said.

"Let me ask you this, Senor Poe...since you resist my analogy. How did you feel when you were an infant and soiled your diaper?"

"I don't remember. But I imagine it felt like shit."

Zee crossed his legs, smoothed the crease of his trousers. "I might be able to remember who I was, to work it out logically, but that would have little meaning. Will it satisfy you if I say I was no one?"

"Might if you tell me who you are now."

"Language has its limits," he said. "When it comes to expressing the inexpressible—the idea of God, the concept of infinity—mathematics is more useful."

"You tellin' me you think you're God?"

Zee's smile widened. "Are you always so literal-minded, Senor Poe?"

"Only when he's bein' a dick!" Lupe tucked her legs up beneath her butt and frowned at me. "You gonna keep bein' a dick, Eddie? Or you gon' let me do my interview?"

I didn't know if she was performing or not. Her fans loved our little spats—they fleshed out our relationship for the simple-minded. But I wasn't in the mood to play.

"Y'know," I said to Zee, "Ramiro's gonna love your ass. Say what you want about him, say he's insane, ruthless, a fuckin' sadist…the man's a sucker for that sound-of-one-hand-clappin' bullshit you been spreadin'. Two of you gon' get along fine."

"I have put substantial proposals before Senor Carbonell," Zee said. "We have a great many topics of mutual interest to discuss. If this were not the case, we wouldn't be meeting."

"Let's hope so," I said. "Otherwise it's gon' be a short night."

●

Fifteen miles out, I could see El Rayo sketching a false horizon as far as the eye could see, a glowing wire stretching east to west. As we drew closer, the taller structures of the city lifted against the fire. The tallest within view was a cathedral that had formerly been known as Nuestra Senora del Rayo, this referring to an apparition of the Virgin that had manifested in the burning red light, witnessed by thousands of the devout. The church had been constructed without a back wall, open to the curtain of fire at the very spot where Our Lady had materialized, just in case She decided to do a second show. It was now a part of the Carbonell compound, organized religion having retreated to safer climes. Ramiro Carbonell and his two sons occupied the rectory, and the two buildings were connected by tunnels and roofed passageways to a dozen lesser buildings, and this warren was segregated from the remainder of Barrio Ningun by high, heavily-patrolled stone walls.

The dirt streets through which we drove were thronged with heavily armed, heavily tattooed young guys. Carbonell affiliates. They moved aside grudgingly as the Rolls nosed toward the cathedral; they flicked lit cigarettes at us, flourished their pistols and spat, then—as we moved beyond them—turned back to their card games and their whores. Pariah dogs cast uneasy glances at us and skulked off into alley mouths; naked toddlers chewing sugar cane and tortillas stood in candlelit doorways and looked on in wonder; teenage hookers tried to peer at the rich people hidden behind the darkened glass. Pastel *casitas* with smoking charcoal stoves; drunks with bloody heads lying maybe dead in front of cantinas with no doors; a beshawled mother lifting a sick baby with fly-encrusted eyelids up to the red light and asking for a miracle. Soon the houses gave out into vast acreage of hovels made of plyboard and cardboard, tires, crates, what-have-you. Thin smoke rose from makeshift chimneys everywhere, like the issue of souls into the body of God: the oily gray cloud they formed overhead. And on the far side, towering above El Rayo like a last holy dream on the edge of hell, stood the cathedral. We could have driven through that place a hundred years before, and it would have been more-or-less the same. Poverty was humanity's most enduring tradition, and Barrio Ningun one of its great temples.

We pulled up beside the compound gate. I stepped out, showed myself to the two guards who stood atop it. "Eddie Poe," I told them.

One of the guards, a guy with some years on him, his chest bibbed with a salt-and-pepper beard, said, "You're good, Poe, but Sammy don't pass."

Behind me, Childers was standing on the running board of the personnel carrier. A couple of raggedy children were staring up at him and giggling.

"I cleared this with Ramiro," I said. "Sammy comes inside, or we head on back."

I gave a circular gesture to Childers. He spoke to someone in the carrier. Dennard, Morely, and Fetisov jumped out and established a perimeter. Childers joined them. The kids quit giggling when they saw Sammy's guns, and the curiosity seekers who had crowded in behind us backed away.

"*Hijo,*" I said to the guard. "Lemme in, or I'm gon' tell Sammy to cut me a new road."

"Think I give a shit about these *putos?*" The guard laughed. "Kill 'em all. I don't fuckin' care."

The street cleared quickly; a handful of tattooed guys remained, too stoned or too stupid to worry about the consequences.

"Three minutes," I told the guard. "Then we're leaving. You makin' the wrong move. Better talk to Ramiro, or you gon' be takin' a ride on El Rayo tonight."

The two guards vanished; in much less than three minutes they returned. "*Bueno,*" said the bearded guy. "*Pasen.*"

The gate rattled back and we drove into a courtyard paved with broken flagstones. A kid in baggy fatigues beckoned for us to pull up by the cathedral steps. The house of God had aquired a post-apocalyptic gloss since the last priest fled. Much of the ornamentation on the face of the building had been shot away or defaced with graffiti; sheets of metal had replaced the stained glass windows, and the white marble steps had been sprayed green, white and gold, and chains of black symbols, like magical equations, had been inscribed atop the paint. From the steeple flew a red banner bearing a black circle. I wouldn't have been surprised to see demons peeking from behind the columns that flanked the carved wooden doors.

Lupe scrambled out and began instructing Frankie to shoot this and that. "We're goin' live again," she whispered to me. "Act like you care!"

Except for our party, the only other person in the courtyard was the kid. He was scrawny, fourteen tops, with shoulder-length hair and a wispy mustache. Large dark eyes brimful of hate. A narrow chin and a beaklike nose a couple of sizes too large for his face. The Carbonell physiognomy. Probably, I thought, a grandson of Ramiro's. He stared at me with a surly hauteur. Even the children were crazy. That's why the Carbonells had risen so high. They outcrazied everyone else.

I told Childers to check out the church. He and Fetisov sprinted up the steps and disappeared inside. Frankie was scuttling across the facade of the building, from broken angel to broken gargoyle, shooting down at Lupe, who was striking poses and delivering her introduction to the Carbonells, telling how Ramiro's fortune, built on kidnapping and drugs, had evolved into an empire founded on vice but with heavy investment in legitimate concerns. Zee stood gazing up at the church. Judging by his contemplative expression, you might have thought he was planning to redecorate. The courtyard was enclosed by high whitewashed walls, some inset with dark doors that led into the family warren. The guards on the gate had disappeared. The sounds of the street were muted. I did not have a good feeling.

Childers appeared at the cathedral door, trotted down the stairs to my side. "The supressor field's on. The minute we got inside, the weapons computers went screwy. Fetisov scanned the place. No trace of noncomputerized weaponry. Felix is packing a knife, but that's not a problem."

"If the supressor field goes off," I said, "you got my permission to fuck 'em up."

Childers shot me a bemused look. "You know what will happen if we waste the Carbonells."

"Nobody's gonna waste anyone. That's why I hired you people. To make sure of that. Even the Carbonell family's not gonna wage war on Sammy."

"Oh, yeah," said Childers, deadpan. "They'd have to be nuts."

"Okay, man," I said, turning to Zee. "It's your party."

He blessed me with a smile, started up the steps. Lupe followed, chattering into her throat mike. Sammy and I brought up the rear.

The Carbonells had gutted the body of the church, replacing pews with a long mahogany Spanish Colonial banquet table and matching chairs; but they had left the altar intact, and it was a sight that might reorder anyone's notion of a benign Christianity. Draped in white silk, appointed with four golden candlesticks and an intricately carved gold chalice, and surmounted by a thirty-foot-tall golden cross. Supported by invisible wires, it appeared to have materialized from the wall of red fire that supplanted the rear wall. The other walls were scorched and pocked with bullet holes. A scent of old explosions hung in the air. Our Lady of Napalm, I thought. *Nuestra Senora de la Guerra Mundial.* The banquet table was situated directly beneath the altar, so close you could hear the hum and feel the heat of El Rayo on your skin. Sitting along one side of it were Ramiro Carbonell, his sons Felix and Ruy, and two guys of about Ramiro's age, late fifties, who I assumed were his advisors.

Ramiro was a big prideful-looking brown-skinned man, his body settling into slabs of fat, with a thick head of sleeked-back gray hair and a bushy mustache. He wore white slacks and a tight-fitting shirt of mauve silk that accentuated the bulge of his belly. Gold rings, chains, a cruxifix. Felix and Ruy were leaner, taller, clean-shaven versions of their papa, but their personal styles were so at variance, they seemed dissimilar. Ruy's dark blue suit made him look like a *mestizo* undertaker, but Felix reminded me of the little stores full of cheap flashy souvenirs I'd passed on the way to Cruzados. He was shirtless, dressed in a black leather vest and matching pants. His chest was adorned with a live ink tattoo that flowed between the image of a rainbow-colored scorpion and what seemed a depiction of a man raping a full-breasted woman. His hair fell in long whiplike braids into which chunks of gold had been woven; his sunglasses were tinted purple, and he probably had on five pounds of chains and bracelets and rings. Whereas Ruy sat straight and alert on his papa's right hand, Felix—on the left—slouched in his chair and affected disinterest in the proceeding. A dozen bodyguards, representative of the tattooed minions we'd seen in the streets, stood a distance behind the Carbonells. Judging by the the anxious way they followed Sammy's every move, I had the suspicion that they felt outnumbered. This set off my detectors. It wasn't like Ramiro to be casual in his attention to security.

Ramiro was all smiles during the introductions, especially when it came to Lupe. "I never miss your show, Senorita Bernal," he said, taking her hand. "It's a great privilege to be a part of *The Border Rose.*"

"*Mucho gusto,*" said Lupe. "You know my associate, Mister Poe."

"We have spoken," Ramiro said, his eyes not straying from Lupe's cleavage. He introduced Lupe to Ruy, who bowed, and Felix, who said nothing, only stared. "Well, then!" Ramiro rubbed his hands together and beamed. "To business!"

Once everyone was seated, Ramiro leaned forward, folded his hands on the table and engaged Zee. "We have studied your economic projections, Senor. All your paperwork. We find it intriguing. But the idea of revolution..."

"Not a revolution so much as an economic takeover," said Zee.

Ramiro did not like being interrupted. "Very well. We find the idea of an 'economic takeover' unnecessary. We control forty percent of El Rayo. As we grow, we will naturally extend our control. Eventually we will run the entire border." He arched an eyebrow. "Why then should we align ourselves with AZTECHS?"

"May I speak freely?" asked Zee.

"Of course," said Ramiro.

"In the first place," said Zee, "the Guzman family and Los de Abajo will contest your expansion. Unsuccessfully, no doubt. But you will lose many soldiers."

"*Hombre!* That's what soldiers are for," said Ruy.

Ramiro nodded approvingly.

"As you say," said Zee. "But you are a business, and every loss, no matter how predictable, how trivial, is a loss. Then there is the matter of legitimacy."

Ruy started to his feet, but Ramiro restrained him with a gesture. "In what way," he said coldly, "do you consider us illegitimate?"

"In the way of nations," replied Zee. "What you are presented with now is a unique opportunity. The south of the country is occupied with the Pan-Mayan

War, and promises to be so occupied for quite some time.

"The central region, including Mexico City, has been drained of resources and wields an empty authority...an authority that cannot withstand a significant challenge. AZTECHS holds contracts with the government that will enable us to neutralize any resistance to the creation of a border state. Even if they could recommit forces now fighting in the south, we can guarantee that they will not have the funds to provision them. In a matter of months you could be not the most powerful man on the border, but the president of an emerging nation. A nation that in a few years will become among the wealthiest on the planet."

"You flatter yourself, senor. AZTECHS technology has changed our lives—revolutionized them—and surely it is a wealthy corporation. But a weathy nation...?" Ramiro snorted in amusement. "What of the Americans? What will they say about all this?"

"The Americans want stability," Zee said. "What causes them alarm is that the warfare among the Carbonells, the Guzmans, and Los de Abajo spills over into their territory. Dealing with one government, not three criminal organizations...this would seem to them an improvement. It would afford them more control of the flow of drugs across their borders."

Ruy made a disgusted noise, and Felix, with marginal animation, said, "Papa, we don't need this shit." Ramiro regarded Zee with a questioning stare.

"Senor Carbonell," Zee said. "You know as well as I the Americans do not want to *stop* the flow of drugs. They merely wish to have a voice in directing that flow. This may eventually reduce the amount of drugs that cross the border, but..."

Ramiro glowered.

"But," Zee went on, "the monies that will come to you as a result of this cooperation will compensate a hundred times over for any loss you experience."

"You're asking us to give up our strength," said Ramiro.

"That's the truth, man!" said Ruy, and Felix nodded.

"Not at all," Zee said. "I'm asking you to temper strength with a restraint born of wisdom. I'm asking to make your entrance on the world's stage."

Ramiro turned to Lupe, who was sitting on Zee's right, doing a whispered commentary, and said, "Quit running your mouth, bitch."

Lupe's voice faltered, then stopped altogether.

Perhaps expecting violence, perhaps merely wanting a wider angle, Frankie scooted off along the table.

"You are asking us to give up our strength," Ramiro said calmly to Zee. "Don't try to persuade me otherwise. A president is not a king. I am a king, and these"—he clapped Ruy and Felix on the shoulders—" these are my princes."

The three of them glared with uniform malevolence at Zee, like three wolves eyeing a dog with a broken hind leg. A silence ensued, one in which the humming of El Rayo seemed to grow louder. I had the idea things were falling apart. Zee didn't get it—he was droning on about the joys of nationhood, oblivious to the fact that the hostile energy in the room had intensified.

"You can earn a significant place in history..." Zee was saying.

"Fuck history," said Felix.

"...by founding a nation," Zee went on. "You can increase your wealth, your power, a hundredfold. And you can do all this simply by agreeing to do it."

"Explain," said Ramiro, still holding Zee with his gaze.

"The instant you agree to the contract, AZTECHS will pay a sum of money into bank accounts belonging to Los de Abajo and the Guzmans. Simultaneously they will cede their interests—in their entirety—to the Carbonells."

"You've talked with them?" Ramiro asked.

"Everything is arranged," said Zee.

"And they have agreed to walk away."

"They're being very well paid to walk away."

"*Cono!*" Felix kicked back his chair and came to his feet; he rested both hands on the table and cursed Zee. "*Pinche cabron!*"

The ragged line of bodyguards shifted in anticipation.

"Wait!" Ramiro gestured Felix to silence, but Felix said, "This is bullshit, Papa! This asshole makes deals behind our backs..."

Ramiro held up his index finger to Felix's face and said, *"Cuidado, chico! Cuidado!"* Felix made a frustrated noise and perched sideways on the edge of the table. Ramiro looked thoughtfully at Zee. "How will all this benefit AZTECHS?"

"Stability," said Zee. "An alliance with a nation state will further guarantee our security."

Ramiro leaned back, worrying his teeth with his tongue. "I assume you are speaking about the security of that thing in the desert?"

"The area we're concerned about is noted in the file we sent you."

Ramiro signaled one of his advisors. *"Dame el filo."*

The advisor reached down to a briefcase on the floor next to his chair and withdrew a folder thick with papers. He slid it along the table to Ramiro, who began poring over it. Ruy leaned in close to have a look. Felix turned his back on the table, walked a few paces closer to the altar and stood staring into the shimmering red light of El Rayo. Lupe asked me questions with her eyes. I shook my head the slightest bit, telling her not to worry. None of my people appeared to have moved. All four men were focused on the Carbonells.

"Tell me about this," said Ramiro, and read from the file: "'With the guidance of AZTECHS, the Carbonell Family will train affiliates to oversee the education of future leaders.'"

Zee began to explain the necessity of purging the Carbonell ranks of the irresponsible and the unstable by filtering them through the process of a sophisticated education designed to equip them to make their way through the straits of international diplomacy. My feeling was that he had Ramiro on the hook—the old guy clearly was entranced by the idea of becoming a world leader. Ruy, I thought, was on the fence. But Felix...Felix was not a guy with whom you wanted to push the notion of purging unstable elements. He put out a vibe like an old fluorescent tube on the fritz.

"What do you think, boys?" Ramiro glanced at Felix, then Ruy. "You want to be a country?" He threw back his head and laughed. "I wonder what we should call it?"

"Let's honor our grandfathers," said Ruy sullenly. "Let's call it Cocaine."

"Whatever you call it," Zee said, "it will be a most remarkable country. It will offer its citizens something no other country can, and this will enable to you hire top people in every field with the mere promise of citizenship. You'll be in a position to achieve economic dominance."

"What are you talking about?" asked Ramiro.

"Your country," said Zee, "will be able to offer its citizens the guarantee of an afterlife."

The three Carbonells met this statement with expressions of incredulity. Finally Ruy said, "You talkin' 'bout that software shit, man?"

"Not at all." Zee seemed to feel a great deal more confident than I did. "It has nothing to do with uploading the personality. I'm speaking of an actual physical place. A Valhalla for the Mexican people. A brave eternity."

Felix made an explosive sound and wheeled up from the table. He mounted the steps of the altar, seized a gold candelabra and hurled it into the fire of El Rayo. There was a faint crackling, a white flash.

"Come back and sit down!" Ramiro told him.

"*No mas, hombre!*" Felix descended the stairs. "I ain't listenin' to this shit." He slapped his chest twice above his heart. "I'm not no damn businessman! I'm a fuckin' *bandido*, man! *Yo soy un criminal!* This is not what the Carbonells do...this pussy bullshit!" He pointed at Zee and walked closer. "This little girl is jerkin' us off with one hand and tryin' to slice off our balls with the other! That what you wan', Papa? You wanna get fucked up the ass by a fuckin' machine? You wanna wear a suit and pretend you fuckin' Napoleon?"

Tears began coursing down Felix's face. The crazy fucker truly loved his family traditions. He was probably seeing himself in the AZTECHS-controlled future, a patriarch reminiscing about the good old days when he used to snuff ten, fifteen people before breakfast. What wasn't so amusing was Ramiro-and-Ruy's reaction. Instead of treating him like a mad dog, they were gazing at him warmly, pridefully, as if his nutzoid act brought back comforting memories of Carbonell atrocities.

"Do it, Papa," said Felix.

He and Ramiro exchanged a meaningful look.

"Do what?" I said, bracing myself on the arms on my chair, ready to jump. "I don't know what you people got in mind, but I recommend caution."

"Felix is right, Papa," said Ruy. "We don't need this."

"I don't know what the problem is," Zee said. "But if you have any doubts, any questions, that's why I'm here."

"What's goin' on?" Lupe came to her feet. "Eddie?"

I hauled Zee out of his chair. "Gentlemen," I said to Ramiro and his brood. "We're leavin'."

Zee shook me off—he was stronger than he looked. "We should all take a moment to reflect," he said, addressing Ramiro. "There is a great deal…" He broke it off and stared at the shimmering surface of El Rayo as if noticing it for the first time. "Run!" he said.

I heard a rumbling, felt the floor shake. Just like in Cruzados, the wall of red fire behind the altar flickered and shut down. I'm not sure how many gunmen were standing on the other side. Enough to make a soccer team. They opened up as I shoved Zee and Lupe toward the door. On my left, Fetisov went down without a cry, and I couldn't understand why we weren't all dead. Then I realized the gunmen must be targeting Sammy, saving the rest of us for hostages, for ransom. They moved into the church, firing century-old handguns unaffected by the suppressor field. The gunfire reverberated, building to a roar, and I lost track of things, focused on getting Lupe and Zee clear. As we passed through the door, Zee took a hit in the back. He stumbled, but kept going. A red splotch like one of those fancy badges attached to Second Prize ribbons bloomed beneath his right shoulderblade.

Childers stood on the steps firing from his hip, spraying the area with micro-grenades from his AR-20, then turning to fire into the church. The courtyard was littered with bodies, flames licking up from their clothing. Dennard threw open the rear door of the personnel carrier, urged us inside. Lupe scrambled into the carrier. Dennard dragged Zee in after her. I opened the passenger-side door, intending to slide behind the wheel, but Childers climbed in the driver's side and kicked over the engine. Bullets plinked off the armored skin. Then we lurched forward, speeding toward the gate. Through the slit windows front and side, I saw Carbonell soldiers scattering. There was a screech of bursting metal as we blew out the gate and barreled off into the wasteland of hovels that separated Barrio Ningun from the cathedral.

Childers made a beeline for the desert, not trying to avoid the flimsy habitations in our path, but cutting a swath through them instead. It was like being inside a whirlwind. Shards of plywood, pots and pans, small appliances, toys, clothing, flapping sheets of cardboard, a woman with a terrified face, all these things and more were flipped up into the air by the passage of the carrier—a surreal form of weather sleeting past the windows, flaring in the headlights. Other lives went down beneath us, discernable as bumps. I tried to yank Childers' arm from the wheel, but he backhanded me. My head cracked against the door. As I struggled to clear my head, I had a glimpse of an intense white flash. A shockwave sent the carrier swerving, veering almost sideways, and I heard a terrible sound. Like something bigger than the world had taken a swallow down into its void of a belly. Then I was slammed forward into the dash. I righted myself and Childers winked at me. "I left Ramiro a little present in the courtyard," he said.

Still dazed, I was unable to speak.

"Just a pocket nuke." Childers spun the wheel and something bulky flattened beneath our tires. "Clean and mean. Two hundred yard radius on the kill zone. We're fine."

I managed to sit upright. "You know how many people you just killed?"

"Thousand...fifteen hundred tops. I thought it might be a good idea to deal with your Carbonell problem. You've got nothing to worry about on that account now."

I peered through the front slit, freckled with the blood of someone we had slaughtered. We had cleared the edge of the barrio and were gliding across the hardpan, heading for deep desert.

"You look like someone stole your bunny rabbit," Childers said.

I made another try for the wheel. Childers pushed me away.

"Take a breath," he said. "They were the bad guys. We should have done it years ago. What's more, you're a hero now. Los de Abajo and the Guzmans, they'll bless your name."

"'We?'" I said. "'Who's 'we?'"

Childers hesitated. "Us," he said finally, and then he spelled it: "Yoo. Ess."

It was obvious that Childers considered himself a humorist. I wasn't certain if he was fucking with me. He was beginning to seem very un-Sammylike. It wasn't so much the comedy as the fact he was acting from forethought—not one of Sammy's strengths.

"Pull over," I said.

Childers gave no sign of compliance.

I drew my gun. "I said pull over, man."

"Sure," said Childers. "Whatever you say, boss."

Before I could react, he snatched the gun from my hand, reversed it and fitted the muzzle to my forehead. The circle of skin it covered went numb.

"Any other orders?" Childers asked. "No? Okay. Then why don't you check on the client?" He nudged me with the gun.

I lifted the intercom speaker from a clip under the dash, thumbed the talk button. "What's happenin' back there?"

Dennard answered, his voice crackling. I thought I heard Lupe in the background. It sounded as if she was doing commentary. "Man's alive, but he's shaky," Dennard said. "He wants to go into the desert."

"Ask him about Morely." Childers pocketed the gun.

I thumbed the button again. "Is Morely with you?"

"He sings in my anger," Dennard said.

"Say again."

Dennard did not reply.

"Guess I'll take that as a negative." I switched off the intercom and sat staring glumly at the pale fissured ground flowing beneath our lights.

"I understand why you're depressed," said Childers blithely. "I mean you really let the team down, Eddie. You should have known Ramiro would have a hole card. Figuring the angles was your job. You were lucky to have me along."

I ignored this, even though it was the truth. "Where'd you get the nuke?"

"Family heirloom."

"Cut the stand-up," I said. "What the fuck is goin' on?"

He spared me a quick look. "You mean ultimately? Or this now?"

"Ultimately will do," I said.

That tickled Childers. He laughed, spanked the steering wheel. "I love a scapegoat with a sense of humor."

"Scapegoat?"

"You're the one in charge. You're responsible for whatever goes down. Only reason you're still alive is so you can take the hit. If you get out of line, I have no compunction against killing your girlfriend. Do you understand?"

"Yeah."

"But I can see you're dying to know," Childers said. "So I'll tell you what's up. I'm going after Montezuma."

"The AI?"

"I know." Childers waggled a hand as if to deflect my smile. "You're thinking what chance does one man have against an AI? No chance at all, right? But you see, Eddie, I am not a natural man." He peeled off his neck patch, tossed it. "The patch is just a boost. I've got more technology in me than all the monkeys in the tree. Montezuma is going to look straight through me. I'm not going to ring one of his bells." His eyes found me again. "What do you care? It's not business, right?"

I shrugged. "Whatever."

"Exactly!" said Childers. "Excellent attitude, Eddie. It'll take you far. Maybe even as far as the good ol' U.S. of A. Would you like that? Would you like it if you and your Pops regained your citizenship? It can be arranged. Just be a helpful lad and do what I tell you."

If Childers thought he could define me as a scapegoat one minute and the next have me buy into a promise of rewards, his technology needed an adjustment. That kind of arrogance was very Sammylike. I decided he must be some sort of mutant Sammy with some new wrinkles designed for this particular operation. And if that's all he was, he had his weak spots.

"Un-unh!" said Childers in a cautionary tone. "Don't you start thinking on me, Eddie. Thinking's dangerous, and we've already seen you're not very good at it."

Week Three

We drove out beyond the stone head, traveling south and west, following the cuts between low hills. Dawn turned to daylight, and I began to see riders on the hillcrests. Never more than three or four at a time. They kept their distance and I could make out nothing about them. Silhouettes against a high blue sky. Then shortly before ten o'clock the carrier's engine died and we rolled to a halt in a wide arroyo bordered by banks of yellow rock. There was no gas problem, nothing mechanically wrong. It simply quit. Childers was unconcerned.

"It was only a matter of time before Montezuma stopped us," he said. "We're inside his first line of defense." He opened his door. "See those patches of glittering sand? There." He pointed to a shoal-shaped patch curving out from a rock face that broke from a hillside. "That's all machines. Trillions of 'em. You wouldn't want to take a walk through it. Likely some of the machines filtered up into the engine and shut us down."

"How you know that?" I asked.

"We know everything."

"'Us,' you mean."

Childers smiled. "Whatever."

We sheltered beneath the overhang of the rock face until late afternoon. Dennard spent the entire time sitting cross-legged, tranced out. With the delicate tattoos on his lips and eyelids, cranes and pharaonic men and women with their arms held in positions of dance, he resembled a serene monster in an Egyptian nightmare. Childers, manly Sammy that he was, declined to take advantage of the shade and passed the hours perched on a chunk of dark rock that thrust up from the sand about fifty feet away, staring out at the desert. Now and again his hand would stray to his pack, as if making sure it was still resting beside his knee. I imagined it contained a program that would shut down but not destroy the AI—if "Us" wanted to kill it, they would have simply nuked the area. Lupe cried and complained for the first hour, then fell asleep. Frankie scuttled about shooting this and that. I tried to sleep, but kept recalling our violent ride through the shanties and wondering how my business would be affected by people believing that I'd nuked the Carbonells and wondering also how the hell I was going to get Lupe and me clear of whatever was about to happen.

Zee lay on an collapsible stretcher that was part of the carrier's medical supplies, fading in and out of consciousness. At one point he beckoned to me, and I kneeled beside him. His skin was acquiring a pastiness, but despite loss of blood and pain, he maintained his calm.

"Senor Poe," he said in a creaky whisper. "Listen to me. This man…" He nodded toward Childers. "You must"—he coughed, closed his eyes—"you must prevent him from accomplishing his mission."

I gave this a moment's consideration. "How you know what's he up to?"

Zee blinked up at me, shaping words with his mouth but making no sound.

"Did Dennard tell you?" I asked. "Is he in on it?"

Very weakly, he said, "What is known to my father, I also know."

"Your father?"

"Please, Senor Poe. Listen." Zee caught at my arm. "If you do not stop him, eternity will be lost."

"Eternity," I said. "Oh...yeah. We can't have that."

Then—thinking that if Zee knew what "his father" knew, I might be able get a line on Childers—I said, "He says the AI can't see him. What's that all about?"

"He is not here. He..." He broke off and concentrated on staying alive.

"You're in contact with the AI, right?" I said. "Can't you direct it to Childers?"

"It is...it's as if my father does not believe he exists." He faded a little, then after about half a minute he went on: "If you are injured, go to one of the organic distribution points. The gates to eternity are all around you."

I'd been feeling scattered before speaking to Zee—this talk of organic distribution points wasn't helping me hold it together.

"So these points, they got a little marker says what they are?" I asked. "'Cause I don't got a clue what the fuck you talkin' about."

Lupe crawled up beside me, leaned in over my shoulder. "Is he okay?" Somewhere along the line she had freshened her make-up and was ready for the camera. The viewing audience would appreciate a nice death scene.

Zee appeared to make a slight gain; a degree of animation had been restored to his face. "What do you know of God?"

I wasn't sure which of us he was addressing, but Lupe jumped right in. "Sundays when I was a little girl," she said, gazing soulfully at Frankie, who had taken a position facing her on the opposite side of the stretcher, "my mami would set out a white lace dress with the ruffled skirt, and…"

She began to relate her churchical experiences, how she flirted with the little boys, especially that cute Pedro Garza, and everyone marveled over how beautiful she looked. It was a total fantasy. Lupe had been brought up in Santa Barbara. Her father was a successful lawyer who spent his Sundays on the golf course, and her mother's hangover rarely permitted her to rise before six in the evening. As far as I knew she had never called her mother "Mami." Slut, bitch, and "that fuckin' old hag…" were the pet names she usually applied. I was starting to wonder if shock had knocked her brain off-line, and she had retreated into her on-air personality.

"Man didn't ask what you wore to church," I said. "What you wore to church and who you wanted to screw when you were twelve don't have a hell of a lot to do with God."

Lupe frowned at me, and I figured we were about to have one of our famous, ratings-boosting fights, but Zee, who was clearly tuned to another channel, interrupted by saying, "You once asked me who I was before I came to the desert. I am now who I was then...but made clean. Perfected."

I was still pissed at Lupe, and my impulse was to tell Zee to save his bullshit for St. Peter or whoever waited beyond the organic distribution points. But the guy was dying. You had to cut him some slack.

"As will you be," he went on. "Both of you."

I could think of worse fates than spouting platitudes and smiling in everybody's face, but not many. Zee's eyes closed, and I thought he had canceled his reservation, but he heaved a sigh and focused on my face.

"Your purpose is more worldly than mine," he said. "But it is no less God's purpose."

"What do you mean by God?" I asked, trying to make the question seem an inquiry and not a bullshit challenge.

Zee's happyface smile widened. "Look around you. You are with Him now."

I saw sand and sage and yellow rock. I saw an iguana scuttling across a patch of ocher sand. God. Why not? I thought. An AI who believed it was God, or God manifest in an AI. Not much difference there.

Lupe put on her professional anchor voice. "Are you suggesting, Zee, that the AI known as Montezuma is, in fact, the entity we think of as *El Gran Senor?*"

"Every age has its avatar," Zee said weakly. "Believe what you will now. Faith is your destiny."

She asked more questions, but Zee said he needed to rest. She gazed at me with wounded devotion, retreating into the persona of the Border Rose. "Eddie! You were mean to me."

I told her to go fuck herself and eased myself down into a more comfortable position. That's when, looking past her shoulder, I spotted the rider.

It was watching us from about twenty yards away, about fifteen feet from the rock where Childers was stationed. At that distance I should have been able to make out considerable detail, but as far as I could tell, there was no detail to see. It looked to be the living shadow of a horse and rider. The human form flowed out of the horse's back. Its movements—the uneasy shifting of the horse's feet, the rider's head and torso turning—made me think of animation. Too fluid to be alive. It stepped closer, halving the distance between us, stirring up puffs of dust. Dennard eased his rifle up onto his knees. Childers might have been wedded to his rock the same way the rider was joined to his mount.

Lupe clutched at my shoulder. I felt I was looking deep inside the rider, that its blackness had infinite depth. My hand went to my gun; then I recalled Childers had taken it. The rider was half-again normal size, conveying an impression of enormous menace and power. Ebony; anthracite; pitch; obsidian; there was no word dark enough to describe its blackness. It sat unmoving for a dozen heartbeats, then wheeled about with uncanny suppleness and trotted soundlessly off along the arroyo. I glanced down at Zee. No surprise there.

He was smiling.

◓

We walked south into the blue-dark night toward
a point known only to Childers. He and Dennard
carried Zee's stretcher. A half moon was sailing high,
and I could see for miles in every direction. The arroyo
had given way to rolling hills and we kept to the
ridgetops in order to avoid the glittering patches of
sand, which had grown more numerous, showing like
sprays of diamond on the valley floors, emerging from
shadow, bordered by slate-blue slices of ordinary sand.
Riders tracked us from adjoining hilltops. There were
more of them now. I saw as many as thirty at one time.
They would parallel our course for a while, then vanish,
only to reappear farther along. Fear pulled at me, but
Lupe was so upset, I forced myself to maintain so as
to reassure her. Childers seemed unaffected, but as
we moved deeper into the AI's turf, Dennard began
to come apart. He took to mumbling what sounded
like prayerful incantations and to grunt. The grunts
were accompanied by twitches that acted to shift the
weight of the stretcher, and this came to annoy
Childers. At length he told Dennard to set the stretcher
down and got in his face.

"Straighten up, god damn it!" he said. "I don't
need you going primitive!"

Dennard gave him a two-handed push and
dropped into a fighting stance.

Childers let out a dry laugh. "You're in my world,
brother. Don't be an asshole."

Dennard shed his rifle and pack, and did an all-over flex. He shifted into a deep crouch, his fingertips grazing the sand. "Come get it," he said. "I ain't followin' no more. I saw my face on that thing in the arroyo."

"Wha-at?" Childers affected a tone of pity such as you might use with a child. "And now you're scared?"

"I ain't scared of you, that's for sure." Dennard flowed into yet another stance, this slightly more upright, with his back straight and right leg forward. "But I'm no damn fool. I know what's comin'."

"You just think you know." Childers shrugged off his rifle and pack. "Christ Jesus! A fucking hallucination, and you go to pieces. In Guatemala I saw beasts made of human shit feeding on the dead. All it did was make me strong. I saw the sun pierced by arrows—I showered in its blood."

"You ain't seen jack," Dennard said. "I was in Zacapas when the black church burned and the demons flew. A hundred brothers saw the same, and they went zero levels, every damn one 'cept me."

They began trading brags, an old pitfighting ritual. I had no thought to get between them. Sammy on Sammy suited me fine. With any luck, they'd scrag each other. Lupe clung to me. Frankie secured a good position from which to shoot the fight. Our ratings were probably off the charts.

The ridgetop we were walking was narrow, with a thirty foot slope, and as the two men grappled, I realized that one or both would probably wind up sliding down the slope, landing among the glittery patches of sand curving everywhere below, standing forth against the darker sand like rhinestone scalloping. For what seemed a long while, neither man earned an advantage, fighting almost silently, with just the sound of their labored breathing audible; but at last Dennard slipped beneath Childer's left arm, got behind him, and applied a chokehold that would have crushed an ordinary throat in seconds. Childers tried to bite Dennard's forearm, failed, gnashed his teeth. His face darkened, and he clawed at Dennard's eyes. I was pulling for Dennard. His attitude toward the mission was more or less my own, and I started thinking how to deal with him once Childers was dead. But then Childers' neck and torso expanded, as if his bones were flexible like a python's ribs, and this loosened Dennard's grip. He spun inside the grip and head-butted Dennard, knocking him to his knees; then he seized the front of Dennard's jacket and hammered him with two chopping right hands. I couldn't believe Dennard was still conscious. Blood and slobber spilled from his mouth. His eyes rolled. But when Childers threw a third right, he ducked it and locked his arms about Childers' waist, lifting him into a shoulder carry. I saw him tense, adjusting the hold, preparing to throw Childers off the ridgetop—but he stepped back, lost his footing, and Childers slipped from his shoulder. Overbalanced, Dennard snatched at the air, toppled and went rolling down the slope, coming to rest directly below. As he lay spreadeagled, dazed, the glittering curves that mapped the desert floor began to flow, spreading in a film to cover a considerable section of the desert around him—watching those bright shapes in motion transformed my anxiety to full-blown fear. The fall had busted Dennard up—it took him twenty, thirty seconds to get to his feet, but by then it was too late. He was standing in a slate-blue circle in the midst of a diamond pond. To escape he would have to walk across a molecule-thin carpet of machines. He looked bad. One arm appeared to be broken, and blood was coming from his mouth. He turned within his confining circle, searching for an escape route. A rider was approaching from the west, coming at an easy trot, looking less like something alive than a horse-and-rider shaped hole in a photomural that was sliding past so as to simulate movement. Lupe began to recite a Hail Mary.

"This is your moment, brother!" Childers said. "Live in it."

The rider stopped ten, twelve feet away from Dennard. They seemed to be regarding one another, but I noticed that Dennard's eyes were closed. It was a compelling tableau. The bleeding warrior with his Egyptian tattoos, death black and empty on its eyeless stallion, and the glittering sand enclosing that blue target circle. I could hear wind troubling the sage, Lupe's whispered prayer, my own hushed breath. Then Dennard let out a scream, as enraged and shrill as a mother eagle sighting a violated nest, and launched himself at death, an assault knife in his hand. The impact should have driven the rider backward, but it didn't even tremble. It looked as if Dennard was half-sunk in a tarpit, his back and portions of his legs and arms emerging from an area spanning from the rider's chest to the horse's belly. Gradually he sank deeper, until his camo-draped butt was the only thing visible. The absurdity of the sight somehow made it more horrifying. Lupe buried her face in my shoulder. Whether she felt any compassion for Dennard, or if she was merely appalled by the thought that his fate might soon be hers, I had no clue.

"Bet that hurt," Childers said with satisfaction, once Dennard had vanished completely.

I wasn't so sure. Dennard had gone still at the instant of impact. The contact might have killed him outright, but if he had been alive, he had not shown the least sign of resistance.

Childers clapped me on the shoulder. "Break's over, Eddie." He gestured at Zee on his stretcher. "Grab an end."

"You crazy? I wouldn't make it a mile carryin' him."

"Amazing what a man can do when he's desperate." Childers fished in his trouser pocket, pulled out something shiny. "But I can help you out."

"Fuck is that?"

He showed me the shiny thing—a syrette. "Sammy."

"Right," I said. "I'm gonna join the freak brigade. Not a chance."

"I'm afraid I'm going to have to insist."

I backed farther away. "Zee's almost dead. What you need him for, anyway?"

"You never know—he might come in handy."

Out of the corner of my eye I saw Frankie shooting me, and I heard Lupe giving a commentary. She was standing behind me, doing her Border Rose on-the-spot-with-this-latest-development thing.

"Bitch!" I started toward her and she darted away.

"Eddie," said Childers reprovingly. "You don't get mad at a snake for hissing."

I ignored him. "Lupe…"

"What am I s'posed to do?" she said tearfully. "I can't do nothin'."

I couldn't tell what was going on with her. Maybe she couldn't tell, either. The spark of emotion that had brought us together was flaring its last beneath the pleats and ruffles of our pretend-lover bullshit. Standing in her disheveled silk blouse, her white slacks, with her hair lifting in the desert wind, she was beautiful and false, a perfect illusion that I had succumbed to. The extent to which I had chumped myself made me feel desolate and uncaring. Why should I worry about her…about anything? I was walking toward death with Sammy. I might as well join him in insanity.

"I'm not asking for volunteers." Childers came forward, doing his Mister Menace scowl, holding up the syrette.

I looked at Lupe for what I figured would be the last time through sane eyes. "Hit me," I said.

●

Childers kneeled beside me as I jabbed the syrette into my arm and stared into my face. "The first time," he said. "It's a beautiful thing."

What he saw, I have no idea. What I saw was everything brand new. Take sand, for instance. It previously had seemed unvarying, uninteresting, but now it had been transformed into a tactical topography, areas of minimal exposure and good footing and so forth. People? I glanced at Lupe and instantly dismissed her as a threat—her face was a mask of weakness and fear. But Zee, though dying, was possessed of a supreme confidence that put me on the alert. I gauged everything in terms of its potential danger to me. Despite what had happened to Dennard, those things I saw that were truly dangerous—black riders, living sand—only supplied my amplified senses with fresh reasons for arrogance. My skin was hot, my heart rate accelerated, yet I felt indestructible. All my senses had been drastically enhanced. Sammy could see a sand-colored spider sitting on rock of the same color thirty feet away, a creature that would have been invisible to that cakeboy Eddie Poe had he been standing next to it. The fragments of Sammy philosophy I'd heard over the years suddenly seemed deep and seasoned ideas, and not the globs of reconstituted Bushido they had once seemed. Whereas before Childers had been somehow pitiable in his strength, when I looked at him now I saw an elder brother who was more adept and powerful than I, not of my blood but a pure relation, one who knew what I knew, who drank from the same reservoir of anger that

I drank from, who heard, as did I, the singing of his blood, the whine of the circulatory system orchestrated into a music of red wires. In the back of my mind a voice was squealing that I had lost it, but after a minute or so I didn't hear it anymore.

"How's it feel to be human, Eddie?" Childers grinned, and I could not help grinning in return. "The stuff they used to hand out to our brothers back when the war started," he went on, "it was hardly more than juiced-up amphetamines. But this"—he held up a pack of syrettes, then tossed it to me—"this is the shit. Gets you there quick and keeps you there." His grin broadened. "You're going to love it."

I had to admit the drug was a perfect complement to our moonlit walk. Carrying Zee proved a snap. I was tireless so long as I shot up every couple of hours. Childers kept up a stream of chatter as we went, some of it designed as taunts, reminding me that I was a subordinate, an inferior, and some intended to help me adapt to the wonderful world of Sammy. Tips on how to focus, how to interpret certain sensory information that I'd previously been unable to perceive. I found I was able to compartmentalize his bullshit, store what was helpful, and at the same time to generate and consider my own thoughts, which were conflicted. I knew I was no more than a tool to Childers, and I understood this was his right—he was my commander by virtue of strength and experience, and I was part of a campaign, thus expendable. But despite buying this to a degree, I wanted to stay alive, and toward that end I tried to come up with a plan for killing him. (Perhaps this dichotomy was in part responsible for the middling success Sammy was having in a war against an outgunned, outmanned populace to the south.) However, I had no luck in developing a plan. I recognized that Childers— accustomed to derangement—could both outfight and outthink me in this condition. All I could do was hope for a circumstance to arise in which he was placed at a disadvantage. It would have to be a hell of a disadvantage if I was to stand a chance. Of course it was possible that the AI would kill him, but Montezuma's plan was even less in evidence than my own.

At dawn we stopped to rest in the shade of an enormous rock that stood by itself on a stretch of hardpan. Shaped like a Go counter, flat on top and bottom, with a smooth bulge all the way around its sides. It did not appear to be a natural formation, but Childers displayed no hesitancy in approaching it, and I deferred to his judgment. Frankie scurried up the side of the rock and disappeared. Lupe collapsed beneath the overhang. We laid Zee beside her. I sat down a few feet away, plucked a syrette from the pack and gave myself a boost. Childers chuckled. I imagined he was still wrapped in nostalgia, hearkening back to the infant stages of his own addiction. When I was done fixing, he said, "All right, people. I'm going to do a little recon, scope things out. I want you to stay right here. You move, and I will know about it. We clear?" Then he strolled off out of sight around the rock.

The sky above had gone the blue of old washed-out jeans, and the hardpan had turned blood red, and the sun, partway up, was already distorted by heat haze, a rippling crimson bubble welling from the horizon, heralded by tiers of low cloud stained mauve, peach, and burnt orange. It—the entire panorama—was like a design on a flag, the one flying inside me, its colors and shapes knitted from the new feelings that were consuming the corpse of my former personality cell by cell, eliminating all but the essence of the human, the basic aggression and will to live that, in everyone but Sammy, had been drowned in softness. It was the emblem of a world in which I was the only thing that mattered. I cared nothing for anyone except for those who might help keep me alive—the trouble was, of the three people with me, I couldn't decide if any of them fit that category. I was calm. Anger was great in me, but I had no need for anger, and I was content to wait for an opportunity use it. To watch the shadowy hills in the west acquire detail and color, and the sky lighten to a frail blue. To feel a hot wind rise in the east an instant before a speckled lizard resting on the hardpan lifted its head in response to that same stirring.

We had been resting for about a half hour when Zee began to talk. Nonsense at first. A few muttered phrases, and he lapsed. Then he started up again with a bit more coherence: "I don't...understand..." He licked his lips, his eyes fluttered open, and he saw me. "The city," he said, and one of those beatific smiles washed some of the weakness from his face. "He has built you a city. And you will build him one."

Lupe was lying on her side, watching him not with journalistic intent, but with the mild curiosity of the exhausted.

"You make perfect mourners," Zee said. "Neither one of you has the capacity to mourn, and truly, there is nothing to mourn." I thought he was about to laugh, but he choked instead.

I had an Eddie Poe thought behind a Sammy-type perception—that Zee had told us the truth, and he was the same man he had always been. As the layers of life were peeled away, I could see he was the same all the way through and that he had been who he was for a very long time. That was what made him dangerous.

A tiny bird winged low overhead, its wings whirring. I saw its throat pulse as it passed, and its black eye glisten.

Zee faded out again, and Lupe once more closed her eyes. A vulture began circling a spot out beyond the edge of the hardpan, one marked by several organ-pipe cacti standing in partial silhouette against the lightening sky. Being Sammy was not without its aesthetic side. I was discovering that I had an appreciation for the desolate, the stark. This may have had something to do with the fact that such landscapes offered relatively unimpeded fields of fire, but I took immense pleasure in the desert view nonetheless—it resonated with my own bleakness of purpose.

Childers had said that we would rest for an hour, but an hour went by and he did not return. My buzz was starting to mellow, so I did another syrette and felt that sweet heart-slamming rush heat my blood, boil away superfluous brain cells. I watched the world reorder into a map of strategic points and values. I heard Zee mumbling, but I was too exultant to care. Eventually I turned to him. His cheeks were sunken, gray. Dark crescents beneath his eyes, but the eyes remained vital, black lakes in a desert of flesh.

"So you are a soldier now," he said in a cracked voice.

This didn't seem to require a response.

Frankie, who had likely registered the sound of human speech, came scuttling down from whatever he had been doing atop the rock and pointed his lens at Zee.

"You will be a fine soldier," Zee said. "But whose soldier will you be?"

Wearily, Lupe hauled herself up to a sitting position. She looked at me, then averted her eyes. She leaned close to Zee and said, "Last night when the rider came to Dennard—I thought you said your father couldn't see us."

Very weakly, a whisper, he said, "They are drawn to death."

Lupe leaned closer, as if to kiss him. "They're independent of the AI...your father?"

"Let him die," I said. Death was something I was coming to respect in that it offered—as it had to Dennard—new possibilities for triumph.

A creaky syllable escaped Zee's lips. It sounded like "gay." His mouth remained open. So did his eyes. Lupe felt for a pulse under his jaw and jerked her hand away. "Eddie," she said, and when I remained silent, she shouted, "Goddamn it, Eddie! Are you in there?"

"What?" I said. I think the shout engaged me on some military level, that I associated shouts with battle mode.

"You got to do somethin', man!" she said. "That *puto* Childers is gon' kill our ass. You got to help me, Eddie!"

Her use of the imperative, too, engaged me. She seemed to be in command. "What do you suggest I do?"

"Fuck, I don't know!" She pushed herself away from Zee's body. "The riders. Maybe we can use the riders."

I waited.

"If they're independent of Montezuma," she said, "maybe we can get 'em to come help us."

"How?"

"That shit you shootin' make you stupid? Think of somethin'!"

A glistening in Zee's left eye caught my attention. As I watched, it became a glitter. Lupe saw it and backed farther away. Within a few seconds, grains of glittering sand began to pour from the eye and down Zee's cheek, forming into a little heap beside him, about the size of an anthill.

Lupe crossed herself.

Once the last grains had issued from the eye, the glittering pile started to flow away from the rock, slowly at first, but gathering speed, until it seemed to zip off toward the south like a little silver snake and was gone. During most of the process I never twitched. No pile of sand was going to kick Sammy's ass—I intended to outface whatever danger it presented. But just before the silver snake picked up speed, acting on impulse, I sliced down with the edge of my left hand, chopping off its tail. I would like to believe the Eddie Poe component of my personality penetrated to the heart of the situation and caused me to act; but in truth I think it was a macho Sammy move that proved to be a brilliant stupidity. The sand grains pushed delicately against my hand, filmed over the palm, and then became inert.

"Scoop 'em up!" Lupe told me, staring at the inch of sand trapped against my hand.

I was not inclined to obey her.

"Dumbass...!" She came to crouch beside me, and using the blade of a penknife she produced from her hip pocket, she carefully lifted them and deposited them on a pocket handkerchief made of the same red silky material as her blouse. Then she knotted the handkerchief and held it out to me. "Take it!" she said.

"What for?" I said.

"Eddie." She pushed her face into mine. "If your pale *gringo* ass is listenin', try and hear what I'm tellin' you, okay? In the handkerchief there's about a million little machines. I don't know why the hell they didn't swarm all over you. Maybe 'cause they come out of

Zee, maybe they know you or somethin'. But if you throw 'em on Childers, maybe it'll fuck him up. Now take the goddamn handkerchief!"

I took it and stuffed it into my shirt pocket.

"You not gon' say nothin'?" Lupe jabbed two fingers at my chest. "You jus' gonna sit there?"

I made no reply, busy examining the potentials of the situation. The idea of going up against Childers with a pocket hanky containing a gram of machine dust did not strike me as wise.

Lupe tried to slap me, but I caught her wrist, squeezed until she cried out. I released her and she pushed herself to a safe distance. A tear held at the corner of her eye, flashing like a live crystal, then slid down her cheek.

"Please, Eddie! Please listen to me."

Her weepy tone did not move me, but then she grew angry again, and though her voice was still freighted with a weaker emotion, I was swayed to listen.

"Goddamn you!" she shouted. "We gotta kill this son of a bitch, Eddie! Y'gotta help me!" She got to her knees, cradling her sore wrist. "You wan' me to tell you I love you? That do it for ya? I don't wanna deal with it, I don't fuckin' need it! But it's true—I love you! I do! Y'hear that, man? I fuckin' love you, okay?"

Beneath the layers of falsity that muffled Lupe's soul was something I had never seen before, a palpable force made visible—it seemed—by her admission of love. Was it love I saw? I don't know. It could have been another of Lupe's games, the operation of some primal falsity. But whatever it was, it was very strong, and its strength along with Lupe's anger not only impressed itself on Sammy, it spoke to the flickering remnant of Eddie Poe and joined those two parts of me in a unity of purpose. Lupe seemed to be changing, acquiring the potency of an emblem, an icon, a soldier's reason for sacrifice. Her eyes were as depthless a medium as the black stuff of the riders. Her cheeks taut with strain, her red lips parted. All her weakness and lying substance appeared to be dissolving away like a skin being shed, revealing a new creature beneath. What I felt for her, Eddie Poe's infantile love and Sammy's chemically sculpted, perverted samurai honor, combined to form a dutiful passion. If Zee had been around, I could have told him whose soldier I was now.

●

As we walked from afternoon into evening Childers' mood was buoyant—Zee's death had been a sort of "Oh, well" event for him—and he told us stories about Guatemala. How his platoon had joined up with a larger force of pro-government Guatemalan troops to overrun a rebel village, killing everyone. After the victory they had found a huge vat of homemade beer— the marines squabbled with the Guatemalans over possession of the beer, and eventually they slaughtered them as well. He told us how Sammy had watched the souls of the dead rise from the battlefield and how he had seen strange anthropomorphic creatures in the jungle invisible to normal eyes. They were slender, very fast, their skins imbued with a chameleonlike quality that allowed them to blend in against the backdrop of bark and foliage. A member of his platoon had killed one, but they had been unable to preserve it. Insects had eaten everything but the bones. Childers had kept a fragment of bone and when he had it analyzed, it proved to be the relic of a human child.

"The citizens might say we shot us a regular kid," Childers said. "What do they know? You spend time in Guatemala, you come to learn that strange is normal in a place like that. The idea that kids could go mutant living in a jungle, it fits in with all the rest."

Frankie scooted ahead, shooting him as he talked, and Childers struck a pose, flexing his biceps.

"One time," said Childers, "we took some R&R in San Francisco de Juticlan, this garbage heap of a town on the Rio Dulce, right on the edge of the jungle. The town had grown out over the river. All these shanties set on stilts, connected by walkways. Most of the people living there were hookers. Pimps, bartenders, gamblers, and hookers—that's all there were. We'd been fighting Angolans the last couple of weeks. Tough bastards. They weren't great soldiers, but they were great killers, and we needed a party. We took over this mega-shanty out from the shore. Two stories, with dozens of interconnected rooms. We lit the place up. Threw all the local tough guys in the river and got working with the women. So anyway,

I'm in a room with my *senorita*—the bitch couldn't have been more than fifteen, but she was an animal! And I heard Jago yell. Jago Wharton. One of my buddies. About six, seven of us found his room and busted in. He was lying on the bed, looking up into a corner of the ceiling and screaming. Terrified. We looked up to what he saw, and Christ! His whore was hanging upside down from the tin roof. Like a goddamn spider. She had black marks on her face—like her skin was splitting open and something was forcing its way out. Somebody shot her, and we pulled Jago together. I don't know what the hell the hooker was. Some kind of witch, maybe. We figured there must be more around, so we gathered up the rest of the hookers and examined them. Found four others just like the first. We were going to shoot them, but Jago"—Childers laughed—"he goes, 'No, man! Don't kill 'em!' And he starts telling us what an amazing ride the first one was giving him before she went into spider mode. It was unreal, he said. So we took turns screwing the other four. We watched them close so they couldn't pull any of their spider shit, and Jago was right. The bitches must have been triple-jointed. You could bend them any fucking way." He laughed again—airily, lightly. "*Almost* any fucking way."

I tried to marry the things I had begun to see— halos around objects, phantom gassy shapes in mid-air, and so forth—to Childers' stories. Would these mild hallucinations evolve into wild distortions of reality? Would I start seeing what Childers wanted me to see? It was hard to believe that he had actually seen the things he said he had, and I suspected that Sammy living at close quarters and under stress might come to see whatever they wanted to see. Such a quality would make the job easier on the conscience, but it didn't exactly prepare you for a return to civilian life. Then maybe there was something to the stories, maybe the world was many worlds that all interfaced in places such as Guatemala, and only Sammy knew their secrets.

I had no opportunity that night to introduce the dust in Lupe's handkerchief into Childers' bloodstream, and I'm not sure I would have taken the opportunity if one had presented itself—it might have been our only chance, but it was too much of a long shot, and I preferred to wait for a significant opening. Soon Childers either ran out of stories or of the urge to tell them, and we went in silence across the moonlit sand. Whenever we stopped to rest, he would sit far away from us or go out of sight completely. During these breaks Lupe made crazy suggestions about what we should do and urged me to come up with my own, but I ignored her and concentrated on focusing myself. I couldn't imagine a scenario that did not involve a physical confrontation with Childers, and I wanted to be ready.

Sunrise brought us to the top of a ridge overlooking a lake of glittering machines with a village of adobe huts on the far shore, a few miles distant. The eastern sky was striped with bands of glowing agate, and the crimson sun was warped by heat haze into a convoluted figure, an Aztec Rose painting the hillsides and silhouetting the saguaro against a pale indigo sky. Childers stared at the village through binoculars for a long time, then handed the binoculars to me. There were thirty-one of the huts. Their shapes were strangely modern, as if they were hotel bungalows designed to reflect a native motif. People moved through the dusty streets. Indians. Most wearing white robes. I spotted a man on horseback. The horse was fashioned of a gray metal that looked to have the flexibility of flesh. Its eyes were raised obsidian ovals and it had obsidian decorations on its face and flanks. The man was holding a long-bladed spear in his right hand; from his left dangled the body of a whiplike black animal with a flat head that appeared vaguely feline. The scene had an atmosphere of ordinary process, but its details were almost entirely exotic, and that dissonance made me uneasy.

"This is it," Childers said, taking back the binoculars.

Lupe, who had sunk to her knees, said, "The AI?"

Childers paid her no mind. "All right," he said to me. "I want you to listen."

My sergeant, my enemy. As he spoke I studied the coarse map of his features, trying to read its microexpressions, and I concluded that for all his bravado, Childers was afraid.

"We're going in," he said. "Give me any trouble, I'll kill you both. Bang! Just like that. No hesitation. Hear what I'm saying?"

I nodded.

He ported his rifle and gave me a cold, steady look. "Whatever you think of me, I'm the good guy here." He gestured at the village. "That thing out there has a plan for us. For all of us. It wants us gone. That's how it intends to guarantee its security. The Carbonells had the right idea. Montezuma wants to take our strength. It wants to be left alone, to do whatever it wants without human intervention. The easiest way to get rid of us is to turn us all into zoned-out freaks like Zee. Is that what you want? I don't think so. You want the right to screw up your life on your own. You don't need a goddamn machine to do it for you. So if you want to keep that right, if you want to return to El Rayo and be Eddie Poe again, then you better remember—I'm the good guy. I'm the hero. You've got two choices. You can die, or you can be a hero, too. Personally, I don't care which choice you make. I've got a job to do—that's all I care about. But you've got some thinking ahead of you."

To the north, several riders were moving along a ridgeline, and Childers tracked them for a second or two. "Fuck," he said distantly, as though speaking to himself. "I don't pull it off, the whole world's going to look like this."

I thought about that, about a world in which you lived on the shore of a machine lake in the light of the Aztec Rose, and rode steel horses in pursuit of shadowy beasts with whiplike tails. It didn't seem so bad, and yet Childers' words about self-determination stirred my blood. I had no real belief in the concept—as far as I could tell free will was as illusory as the patch of dark mist that currently troubled my vision. You made the best of what life handed you, yet you never really understood what you'd been handed. For that moment, however, I wanted to believe in it.

"They should nuke the motherfucker," said Childers. "So what if the economy collapses! It's the only sure way."

He dragged the butt of his rifle in the sand and studied the depression it had made. Frankie scuttled close to get an angle on his face, and I realized how many people must be watching our act. Did they believe we were actors in an End-of-the-World skit? Or were they on the edge of their seats, recognizing that their fate might be up for grabs. Most of them were probably just tripping on the imagery, or thinking about switching to the soccer game, or hoping Lupe and me would get nasty before they had to go to work.

Childers flipped his rifle into the air and caught it by the barrel with his strong right hand. He grinned so hugely, his sargeant's stripes almost disappeared into the leathery folds of his skin. "Aw, hell! Let's go have some fun!" he said.

●

No one noticed Childers enter the village. He set about exploring the place, and the Indians in their white robes would have walked right into him if he hadn't stepped out of their way. But they saw Lupe and me as we approached and came out to meet us on the edge of the machine sea. They all had smiles like

Zee, and their speech was rife with platitude and beatific evasion. They were, I decided, the blessed. They had exchanged the illusion of free will for the illusion of peace. They treated us as if we were long-lost members of the tribe, touching us gently, offering food and drink, letting us bathe, and finally ushering us to our own bungalow, a structure not of clay but of reddish brown stone shaped by tools that had left no mark, and inside a cool dark space with a white bed and a kitchen and soft chairs. Then they left us alone. Exhausted, Lupe fell out on the bed. Frankie perched beside her and began displaying footage of our journey on the wall. I sat in one of the chairs, wondering if the village was Montezuma's demonstration model of machine bliss, what he would do for mankind, or if it was simply a casual, off-handed thing, the AI's way of dealing with some ants he had discovered in his back yard. My mind was thronged with images from old films about evil computers who had attempted to enslave humanity, but Childers' notion that the AI wanted to be left alone seemed a much more reasonable representation of what an intelligent machine would want. If Montezuma had played geopolitical and corporate chess in order to position himself so he could then convert the world to that ol' time religion with a brand new twist…well, that made sense, too. Religion had always been the most powerful weapon in the human arsenal, its effectiveness tested over the millennia, and the AI's version, enforced by its microscopic apostles, would be lapse-proof, heretic-proof. Once in the fold, you'd be there for good. Maybe

Childers *was* the good guy, I thought. Maybe I should be helping him instead of plotting to kill him.

Late that afternoon, Lupe sat up in the bed and said, "Shit! Eddie, c'mere!" Then, to Frankie, she said, "Play that last section back."

The images on the wall flickered backwards, steadied, then rolled forward. Frankie's footage showed Childers walking away from the camera into a defile of yellowish rock—it resembled the landscape close to the big boulder beneath which Zee had died. Childers moved along the defile for a couple of hundred yards, then stopped and began stripping off his clothes. He glanced back toward the camera, and Frankie ducked into cover, the footage showing a close-up of a rock. When Frankie peeked out again, a naked Childers was exercising. Doing Tai Chi. I saw nothing that would have excited Lupe. But then his movements became more extreme, and I understood what she had reacted to—Childers' body was changing as he worked out, expanding and contracting with the fluidity of a serpent's body. The camera zoomed in on his face. There were distinct glitters in his eyes that did not appear to be the result of reflected light.

"Magnify one of the eyes and hold," Lupe said. And when Frankie did as ordered, she told him to roll it in slow speed.

Magnified, the eye was proof of Childers' technology. The glitters in Zee's eyes had possessed the same inorganic luster and accumulated with the same rapidity.

"Okay," Lupe said to Frankie. "Normal speed and range."

Childers began to clamber about the rock walls with the agility and quickness of a monkey. I saw that I had absolutely no chance against him in a fight, and this reinforced my feeling that I should align myself with him. Sick fuck though he was, half-machine though he might be, he was likely the closest thing to a good guy in the scenario. But when I made these thoughts known to Lupe, she became angry. "Jesus...Don't you get it?" she said. "The government don't have the technology to do somebody like Childers. AZTECHS is the only one can manufacture that kinda shit."

"What're you sayin'? Montezuma's using Childers to off himself?"

"Your brains musta melted. It's another AI, Eddie. It's gotta be. Another machine's tryin' to take down Montezuma. Childers is workin' for another AI."

"Maybe...I don't know."

"C'mon, Eddie! Think! This whole thing about Montezuma being afraid of the Americans...it's bullshit! If America was going to wipe him out, they woulda done it the second they found out where his mainframe was. The only reason they wouldn't have done it was if they couldn't."

I still didn't understand.

Lupe gazed at the ceiling and said with disgust, "Jesus!" Then she said to me, "Look, man. An AI full of American military secrets, codes, all that, takes off and hides itself out in Mexico. Typical American reaction would be, Kill it. But they didn't kill it, they left it alone so it could gain more power. Only reason they'd ever let that happen is because Montezuma's already co-opted the government. Congress, the President, generals...I betcha every damn one of 'em's fulla of little glittery machines. Just like Zee. And the enemy Montezuma's afraid of, whoever sent Childers...it's gotta be an AI who's escaped the same as him."

What Lupe said made more sense than my theory. If it was true, there were no good guys left. That, too, made sense.

"What're we gonna do?" Lupe didn't appear to be asking me. It was a question asked of the air, the desert, of whatever god—self-anointed or otherwise—that might be listening.

She jumped to her feet, ripped a blanket off the bed and made for the door. "I gotta get out of here!"

I asked what was wrong.

She waved at the smooth reddish brown walls "Where are we, Eddie? What the hell is this place? I wanna be somewhere I know where I am!"

I followed her and Frankie out onto the hardpan to the north of the village—I had no one else to follow and Lupe seemed to have more of a handle on the situation than I. She walked for about a quarter-mile and then spread the blanket and sat down. The sun was lowering, the desert going orange—the fissures in the hardpan had filled with shadows, so it looked as if Lupe and I were situated at the spot where all the cracks started and spread throughout the world. I stood by a corner of the blanket, scanning the horizon. There was no activity in the streets of the village, and no sign of Childers. Off doing one of his techno-workouts, probably. No significant movement anywhere. After a while I sat and stripped off my shirt. I was sweating profusely, a sick drug sweat. I did a syrette and felt instantly better.

Lupe gave me a considering look. "I want you to make love to me. You up to it?"

"I don't know."

"I want you to try!" she said vehemently, petulantly. "I want you to fuck me like you mean it. And I'm talkin' 'bout you, Eddie. Not Sammy."

Put that way, I felt commanded, obliged. It was strange, at first. I wasn't really into it. But as we became more deeply involved, ol' horny, lovelorn Eddie Poe made his way up through the halls of Sammy and took partial control. The sunlight oranged Lupe's body. Orange like the picture of another desert I once saw in a magazine. Gobi orange. My thoughts were moving sluggishly, and the word "Gobi" stuck in my head, making a bloated orange sound. The smoothness of Lupe's skin, unnaturally soft to my enhanced senses, also had a sound, a silky whisper beneath my fingers. We made love for a very long time, while Frankie recorded us for later transmission, riding the sunlight down into crimson and gone, a slow desert fuck that rang crazy changes in my head. One minute I was all Sammy, dutiful in my attentions, noting Lupe's increased respiration and various other reactions; the next I was uncoiling with her, her damp downy patch just the opening of our show, boyfriend-girlfriend deep and dissolving into one another, mainlining emotion. At times I found myself locked between these two states, involved and uninvolved, and I would have odd thoughts that I saw as neon letters against my mental sky, only one of which I can recall—What If The Increase Of the Kingdom Were The Only Significance? The rest were incoherencies. When I looked into Lupe's face, I could read all the feelings she had been hiding from me—they were so clear, it was as if there were words written in Spanish at the corners of her eyes.

Afterward we lay embracing for what must have been an hour, watching the sky go purple and starry, the half-moon slipping up to hang a yin-yang sign above the eastern hills. We had never done that before, never experienced a post-coital coziness—it had always been Okay, let's get on with business—and even though I would go off to a Sammy distance every so often, alerted by a night-sound or reptilian movement, I had no thought of leaving her. She fell asleep, and I continued to hold her, faithful as a dog on drugs. Eventually, convinced that we were secure, I also fell asleep. The waking dreams I'd been having, flashes of border life, red midnights in which I walked hand in hand with Lupe, easy with her...they flowed seamlessly into a more intricate dream of a similar character. We were on Calle 44, near La Perfidiosa, the blacklight inferno dancehall where I hung when I was fourteen, looking for tourists to rob. Everyone was watching us. Whores, hustlers, vendors. They were smiling and calling out, as if proud of us for some reason, and overhead the red fire of El Rayo no longer seemed a barrier, but a hot fundamental sky beneath which I had come to my maturity.

●

I fell asleep in the desert, but I waked in a garden, one of such splendor and expanse, I thought I must still be sleeping. Lupe and I were lying among tall grasses beneath a ceiba tree, its boughs looped with epiphytic vines, and the vines studded with orchid blooms. A broad path paved with fieldstones ran past us on our left, and I heard water running close by. Among an arrangement of fruit trees and flowering shrubs, I saw a clearing with a wooden bench. The air was cool and sweetly scented, and the village was hidden by the foliage…or else it had been magicked away. When I realized the garden was real—real enough, at least, to defy my disbelief—I fumbled in my pants for a syrette and jabbed it into my thigh. Once the rush subsided, I got to my feet and stepped out onto the path. It led between ranks of ceibas toward an Aztec pyramid with a crumbling facade. A smallish one. I reckoned the roof crown to be no more than fifty feet high. The entrance was guarded by two statues of feathered serpents, their features much eroded.

I shook Lupe awake, helped her to stand. As soon as the cobwebs cleared, she became disoriented, terrified of the place, and once that fear had abated, she started fretting about Childers, wondering where he was and what we should do.

"He's around." I said. "Chances are he's here already. But we can't worry 'bout that. We need to figure out what the fuck we're gonna do."

I doubt this made here feel any better, but as we approached the pyramid, she began instructing Frankie on what to shoot. We proceeded cautiously, casting glances to either side, seeing no other living soul or thing. No birds or insects or lizards. The place was a still life. It had the pleasant vacancy of a foyer, an environment designed to admit life, but not to be lived in. I was no expert, but the pyramid appeared authentic in its disrepair. The stones were bleached gray, the edges of the separate blocks were worn round, and between the feathered serpents lay chunks of rotten stone that might have fallen from their folded wings. One touch of the inauthentic was a word carved into the lintel above the door: AZTECHS. Beyond the door a darkened corridor led inward. Lupe thought we should explore the other sides of the pyramid, but I said that if we weren't going inside, we might as well leave.

Childers settled the argument for us.

He came walking around the side of the pyramid, carrying his rife and pack in one hand. The sun gleamed on his stubbly head, and despite the coolness, he was sweating heavily. "I can't find the way in," he said with some frustration. "You have any luck?"

Since we were standing at the top of the stairs, in the shadow of a doorway, I found the question puzzling; but Lupe, apparently, did not.

"There's no door around back?" she asked. "We were just goin' to go look."

He stared at us, chuckled, set down his pack and rested the rifle against it. Then he climbed the stairs toward us. "You're fucking around with me. It's here, isn't it?"

"Right behind us," I said. "Can't you see it?"

He stopped on the top step and stared at me flatly. "No, I can't."

"You should go on in, man. It's wide open."

He studied me, those three wavy lines on his forehead deepening.

"What's inside?" he asked.

I stuck a hand in my pocket, fingered a syrette, and jabbed it home through the fabric. Montezuma, I thought, had incorporated something into the door's design that blinded Childers' micro-buddies to its presence the same way Montezuma was blind to Childers. It was the disadvantage I had been hoping for. It stood to reason that if Childers couldn't see the door or the corridor, he wouldn't be able to see anyone standing inside.

"How many more fixes have you got left, Eddie?" Childers asked. "Doesn't matter. Shoot the whole bunch, I'll still kick your ass."

I must have hit a big capillary, because the rush slammed my heart and made me wobble. "It's cool," I told Childers. "There's nothin' there. Just an empty corridor."

He studied me again, indecisive. "You go first."

"I got no reason," I said. "Go ahead, man. Do your little trick."

"All right." He began to unbutton his camo blouse. "We'll handle this your way."

I hoped putting up a front might slow him down. "Know what I figured out?" I said. "You're the same as Zee. You're doin' your Master's work. 'Cept you're like Zee's evil twin."

"Evil? Please! My employer is a friend to all mankind. He likes to poke his finger in and stir up the anthill now and then. But he loves the little critters." He winked at me. "You believe me, don't you, Eddie?"

His chest was hairless, massive, signified by what must have been at least a hundred tattoos of identical cartoonish red ants with goofy popped eyes and oversized feelers. He glanced down at them, apparently admiring their profusion. I took the moment to extract Lupe's handkerchief from my shirt pocket. I hid my hands behind my butt, worked on the knot in the handkerchief.

"Room for a couple more," Childers said, patting his chest. "Then I'll have to start putting them on my back."

I emptied the sand into the palm of my right hand and I closed my fist tightly around it.

Childers did a bodybuilder flex for my benefit. It was impressive, but it didn't affect me. Though I was afraid of pain, I had no fear of death. That's what I was here for, ultimately. Things were very simple. I had a plan, and Sammy with a plan....I felt like my own god.

When Childers rushed me, I pushed Lupe through the door and hurried after her. Childers broke off his charge about six feet beyond the door, baffled. I wanted him to come close so I could get in a clean strike. I was confident in every regard. I would kick him in the groin and hit him with the dust. Then I would keep on kicking him.

"Eddie!" he shouted, and edged closer.

I whispered to Lupe, "Stay here...whatever happens."

"What you gon' do?"

"Just stay here!"

Childers shuffled forward, a couple of baby steps, his hands held out before him, fingers slightly curved. He pushed at the air, and it looked as if he thought he had met with some unyielding surface. His face was contorted with fury and he shouted, "Eddie! Where the hell are you?"

I launched my kick.

Later I came to realize that Childers had anticipated my tactics and was standing well back from the boundary that delimited his vision and must have seen my leg emerge from what looked to be a wall of gray stone; but at the moment I couldn't understand what had gone wrong. He caught my leg, dragged me down the stairs and kicked me in the stomach as I tried to stand. He slammed an elbow to the side of my head, kicked me a second time in the side. He leaned down, grabbed my shirt, and said, "I'm going to break your back. Then you can lie there and watch me tear your bitch apart."

I was so dazed, I couldn't muster a reaction. I knew what he was talking about, but at the same time I wasn't sure what had happened or if he was talking to me. I think he was about to carry out his threat when Lupe sailed in from somewhere, jumped onto his back and rode him to the ground, her arms tight about his neck. She shouted something I heard as "And!" Then they rolled out of sight. After a second I heard a truncated scream. My head had cleared to a degree. I wanted to get up, to find out if Lupe was all right, but I was having trouble breathing. From the pain in my side, I suspected Childers had cracked one of my ribs. He hove into view, standing over me. "So much for Plan A," he said. "Huh, Eddie?"

Sand, I told myself. Lupe had said, "Sand." My right fist was still partly clenched. I could feel the sand in it. I felt it seething against my palm.

"What's beyond the door?" Childers asked.

"Instant death," I said.

"Tell me straight."

"A sandwich shop. They got great chimichangas, man."

Childers squatted beside me, grabbed my shirt front again and hauled me up to a sitting position. "Eddie," he said. "I'm not going to waste any more of your time with threats. I'd prefer to lobotomize Montezuma, but I'll blow the mother up if I have to. So I don't really need you, man. You understand me?"

I brought my right hand up to my forehead, as if to rub it, a weak, faltering gesture, and with a flicking motion, I threw the sand into his eyes.

Childers let me fall, rubbed his eyes, cursed. He felt his way over to his pack, pulled out a canteen. As he tipped back his head and flushed out his eyes with water, I struggled to my feet. Pain stabbed my side, but when I jabbed myself with two more syrettes, the rush washed pain away. My heart was doing polyrhythms, and I was probably close to ODing. But my confidence was supreme—Childers didn't have a prayer. Sammy was in charge of the situation. That the sand had failed to do its job didn't worry me. I could read Childers' muscles. I could predict his every move before he made it.

"That was it?" he said, turning back to me. "I knew you had something working, but that was it?" His eyes were reddened, but he seemed fine otherwise. He came toward me, shaking his right hand as if to free it of tension. "Sorry," he said, and hit me with his left, a straight jab that left my forehead stinging. I staggered back, and he hit me again with the same punch. I wasn't doing such a good job of reading him anymore. His speed was inhuman. Flick. Another shot caught me on my forehead. The skin there was starting to feel puffy, inflated. I summoned all my focus and saw the next one coming. I countered his intent, stepped to the side and landed my right hand on his jaw just as he threw another jab. I kept throwing punches, a flurry that backed him up but—though I hit him cleanly several times—didn't knock him down. A bruise was developing on his cheekbone. Blood trickled from a nostril. He looked amused.

"When I got to Guatemala," he said, and shook me with yet another jab, "I was just a kid. They transported me into the jungle near the old ruins at El Tamarindo, and I joined up with a small force that had been fighting together the better part of a year." He cracked me again. "Their shit was completely out of control. There was a Mayan pyramid near our camp. A little one. Wasn't much left but a pile of stones. They'd painted it all crazy and tricked it up with a bunch of beaner skeletons lashed to poles sticking out from the sides. It was like their altar." He hit me with a combination that left me spreadeagled. "Things got slow, they'd use the pyramid to play King of the Hill, and this one guy, Corporal Rusedski, Corporal David Rusedski, he won most of the time. He kicked my ass every day for a month, and I got fucking sick of it. It wasn't the ass-kicking that bothered me as much as Rusedski himself. He was Sammy, but he had this citizen streak in him. There was a village nearby, and Rusedski would visit it and befriend the Indians. Give them food and supplies. Play with the children. Everybody saw this as a betrayal. We were brothers. We hated everyone but each other, and Rusedki's charity work seemed a violation of principle. But we were afraid of him, so he just kept on doing it."

I got to my hands and knees and Childers put me back on the ground with two right hands, the second smacking into my temple and making me groggy. He was, I noticed, slowing down. But then so was I.

"One morning before we were scheduled to play King of the Hill," Childers said, "I went into the village and captured a family. Mom, Pop, a couple of kids. I staked them out on top of the pyramid. See, Rusedski really pissed me off. I was new to Sammy, but I loved it, man. It was me. It was where I'd always wanted to be. And Rusedski was a distraction. He was messing up how I felt—how I wanted to feel—with all his bullshit kindness."

The remainder of Childers' story, his revenge against Rusedski, the slaughter of the innocents, how he became King of the Hill...I was taking such a beating, it came to seem like a bloody dream I was having. I saw the family burning atop the barbarously defaced ruin, Rusedski maddened and falling prey to a simple trick, his subsequent torment, as if I were part of those events and not involved in what was actually happening. I caught sight of Lupe every so often. She was alive, trying to stand, but she wasn't making much progress. These glimpses inspired me to fight back, but the fight was essentially over. Childers pounded me about with the ease of a tiger swatting a bobcat...though he had slowed considerably. I could see the punches coming, but my arms might have been bags of cement, and I couldn't take advantage of the openings. I derived no encouragement from his slowdown. It might be that he was merely taking his time. And if the machine dust I'd thrown in his eyes was working on him, I didn't believe it would finish the job before I was finished.

"Reason I'm telling you this," Childers said, walking around me as I stood wobbly and dazed, trying to bring him into focus, "is I don't like you. It's not that you remind me of Rusedski. He was ten times the man you are. You're nothing but a little punk hustler...but you've got that citizen streak in you. I really hate that, you know. I hate when people aren't true to themselves. When they refuse to admit what total bags of shit they are. So what I'm saying, Eddie...This is personal."

He knocked me back against the side of the pyramid, and as he stepped close, I wrapped my arms around him. It was reflex. I had no strategy, I just wanted to stop the punching, but Montezuma must have seen it as his opportunity to get involved, deducing—I supposed—that I had wrapped my arms around his enemy. I had a deathgrip on Childers, and as we stood swaying together, birds descended from the sky and began to peck and claw at us. I have no idea how many—hundreds, I think. Maybe more. And I'm not completely sure if they were birds. I heard their wings and felt their beaks, and they smelled dirty. But I had closed my eyes against the attack and never saw them.

Childers' chest swelled to impossible proportions, breaking my grip, and he rolled away. I fell to the ground, face down, covering up as best I could. Even after Childers had put some distance between us, the birds kept pecking at me for a minute or two. If this was all the defense that Montezuma was capable of, I couldn't understand why his enemy hadn't already taken him out. Then I had one of those neon-letter thoughts like one I'd had the previous night, albeit more garbled, something about the expansion of kingdom and something else about my place in it. I didn't get it. When the birds left and I sat up, blood trickled into my eyes. There were wounds on my face, my neck and hands. I fell back against the side of the pyramid, slumped onto my side.

"That was pitiful," Childers said, walking toward me. He had cuts on his face and hands, too, but not so many as mine. He shouted at the pyramid. "You hear me! That was pitiful!" He looked at me—fondly, it seemed—and drove the point of his boot into my side. The pain was a knife thrust, going deep. I heard a lung puncture, the hiss of air escaping inside me.

"What's beyond the door?" he asked.

My eyes were squeezed shut, and each breath made me wince. "It's a fucking corridor...I told you!"

"Hey, I think your girlfriend's ready to check out," Childers said. "You want to take a look?"

He turned me onto my uninjured side with his foot. Lupe was lying on her back in the grass about ten feet away. Her eyes were open but she wasn't moving. Blood filmed her mouth. Grief and rage possessed me in equal measure. I rolled onto my belly, preparing to stand, and registered something black passing among the trees behind Lupe. Childers caught me by the collar and hauled me upright, spun me about to face him, holding me at arm's length. His pupils were dilated, and his lips stretched in a grin. A spray of blood stippled his cheeks—either mine or Lupe's.

"What's beyond the door?" he asked.

He no longer had any leverage with me—I spat in his face.

Childers broke three of my fingers. The shock made me scream, and I blacked out. When I regained consciousness I was staring up through the crown of a ceiba tree. Eye trash confused my vision. My head felt like a bead strung on a thrumming white-hot wire.

"What's beyond the door, what's beyond the door, what's beyond the door?" Childers made a song out of it, and after a moment's thought, he added a new lyric. "It really doesn't matter, 'cause Eddie's going to die."

Then his brutal features grew slack, confused.

"If you…" He stumbled away, put a hand to his throat. "I don't…what did…" He stood wide-legged, clutching his throat now, and took a clubbing swing, as though striking at an invisible enemy, and began to choke. He went heavily to his knees, still clutching his throat.

It took me a while to stand, and by the time I succeeded, Childers had toppled onto his side. Without the birds and the delay they had caused, I realized, I would be dead. I limped over to Childers. The machines were doing their work at a quicker pace. One of his hands was convulsively opening and closing, and his eyes were bugged. The muscles of his chest twitched, making it appear that the tattooed ants were in agitated motion. Tremors passed through his limbs. His mouth was open. I believe he was trying to scream. I doubted he realized I was there, and I wanted to hurt him, to let him understand that I was enjoying the spectacle. But I couldn't think of anything to add to what was happening. Glittering grains of machine life were swarming up from the grass. They filmed across his body and began to consume him. Bloody rents materialized in his skin, muscle strings were exposed and eaten away, as if by acid. His feet drummed the ground, his neck corded, and he made a fuming sound. If it hadn't been for Lupe, I would have been a happy man. I turned away from Childers to tend to her and saw one of the black riders looming above her.

Some things just own you. They're simply too big for your brain to fit around. They steal your mind and heart, they stop your thoughts and freeze your limbs, and they just own you the way the sight of Lupe and the rider owned me. The rider was a huge black silhouette that had been burned through the paper on which the AZTECHS pyramid behind him was printed, and Lupe lay bloody-mouthed and broken, tiny beneath him. It was as if I were seeing it over and over again. Light burned the image into my eyes, and then the image was reconstructed inside my head and grew too large to contain, and then I was forced to re-see and re-reconstruct it, as if it embodied some fact too alien for my senses to interpret. Each time this happened, I felt more vacant and lost. I had no context for the sight, emotional or otherwise, yet it exerted a pull. I dragged myself forward and dropped to my knees beside Lupe. She was still alive. Her breath was labored, and she was straining to speak.

"Gay..." she said.

I realized this was the same syllable that Zee had spoken right before he died, but it wasn't until afterward that I put it together with the word "gates," with Zee's declaration that the gates to eternity were all around us, and the stuff about organic distribution points. What I did, I did because I had nothing else to do, and no reason left not to do it. Lupe was dying, and I was so busted up and broke-minded and stoned on death, I didn't care what happened. I glanced at the rider. He leaned down, displaying that eerie, fluid suppleness, and extended his black hand—it was fingerless, a big mitten of negativity. I could see forever into his chest and the dome of his head. Eternity minus stars and Bible stories. It looked at the time like a fine place to be. With only the slightest hesitation, and also with the sense that a terrible sadness was preparing to spike in me, I gathered Lupe to my chest and reached out to take the rider's hand.

●

It was like being switched off, then on, then off. Blankness.

Then I would see something, think something.

And then blankness again.

The on-off process went faster and faster until it felt as though I were strobing in and out of consciousness. I don't remember much of what I saw, and I felt as objective as Frankie, removed from the tactical observances of Sammy and the less rigorous perceptions of Eddie Poe. First it seemed I was suspended high above a yellowish white plain, mapped by hedgerows colored bright green and magenta, all laid out in the manner of a garden. The patterns of the hedgerows, intricate as circuitry, were in a state of flux, changing constantly, reshaping themselves. I tried to think, to announce to myself what I was seeing, but all that came to mind were streams of images, scramblings of conception and word. Escaped down the incarnations. The incarnadine boulevards. Efflorescing crystal kingdoms of pure expansion. The expansion of kingdom is the only significance. Things of that sort. Identical to the sort thoughts I'd had when I was making love to Lupe out on the desert. They seemed important but essentially incoherent, and I wasn't sure if they were my thoughts or Montezuma's. I had the idea I was seeing a basic structure, an evolving template upon which the kingdom was founded. I *was* in a kingdom—I knew that much—and I was somehow integral to its expansion, but what that portended in real terms, I had no clue.

After the strobing stopped, I believe I was shown sections of the kingdom. I had a sense that the totality of the structure, which I couldn't fully comprehend, had qualities in common with a beehive or a crystalline formation, hexagonal volumes in close contact, and that it was being displayed for me cell by cell. On several occasions I saw people, each in their own environment. One of them was Dennard. He was standing with his eyes closed at the center of what appeared to be a temple with columns but no roof. Soon it all started coming at me too quickly, and my mind wilted under the assault of light and color and image, and at last there was a light so bright it penetrated my eyelids and burned through me, illuminating me within and without, so that I became almost insubstantial, myself no more than a pattern and part of that patterned place. I lost track of seeing, of feeling, and finally of being...and then I was with Lupe again.

I was still holding her gathered to my chest, but she was not dying, she was very much alive, and we were making love...really making love, not going halfway as it had been on the desert, but totally immersed in one another, every inch of liquid friction, every kiss, every drop of sweat, a kind of speech. We were lying on a bed inset in a marble floor. There was no ceiling, and high overhead was the template of the garden that had been my first glimpse of the kingdom—it flowed above us with the speed of clouds in a strong wind. The kingdom, you see, was under construction. Skies had not yet been installed. That, too, was something I knew. There were no walls, either. Only the floor...though from its edge you could see a city against a field of darkness, its lights stretching away on every side and from horizon to horizon. We might have been in the midst of El Rayo, except the red fire of the border was nowhere in evidence. But I was too focused on Lupe to give it more than a passing consideration.

There were still barriers between me and Lupe, matters of personal history and distrust, but they weren't important to the moment, and in the act of love we came to look so closely at one other that differences and barriers and the concept of distance itself seemed elements of the geography of a country we had left behind. The things she said to me in her passion were things I might have said—she said them for us—and when I pulled her atop me or turned her onto her side, I was enacting the mechanical principles of our singular desire. Nothing is perfect. No object, action, or idea. Yet in the brilliant ease and intensity of our union we felt perfected, we felt each other give way completely in the service of a heated oblivion where we lived a certain while. I remember there was music, and yet there was no music, only whispers and breath and the background drone of some machine hidden beneath us, whose cycles came to have the complexity and depth of a raga. I remember a soft light around us that likely did not exist, or else I do not know how it was generated, other than to speculate that our skins were aglow or weeping melanin. What did exist, what was made of us, what we were for that time...Love's creature lives beyond memory. I only recall its colors.

We lay for a while embracing; we spoke only infrequently and then it was no more substantial than the communication of animals when they settle next to one another, issuing comforting growls. Soon we became lazily involved, and as we moved toward completion, I experienced again the brilliant light that earlier had burned through me. This time it illuminated us with the intense clarity of an X-ray, and I saw how beautiful we were, how we had discarded the myths of ugliness, the false shroud of imperfection. I imagined our perfect skeletons picked clean of flesh and set out for display—advertisements for god. When I looked at Lupe, it seemed I was looking along the corridor of her life, past the career-business hustle, past the legend of her youth and the lie of her fairy tale princess childhood, past moments like stained glass windows and others like boarded-up doors, past tics and tempers, minor disorders, all the pointless behaviors that seek to define us, and I saw her as she might hope to be seen, the true thing in her revealed. Whether what we had become to one another was a side effect or part of Montezuma's plan, it was what I wanted, and I didn't care how it had come to pass.

As I lay there afterward staring up at the fake sky, I recalled what Papa had said a few nights before about my having no future, how he had been right—albeit not sufficiently expansive—in his judgment. It seemed fairly certain that none of us had a future. Montezuma would see to that. Glittering machines purifying us and scouring us clean, wedding us to holy purpose, as Lupe and I had been purified, scoured, and wedded. Though I didn't understand its particulars, I could feel the shape of new purpose inside me. But I did not feel like Zee had appeared to feel. Blissed-out and babbling biblespeak. I felt like Eddie Poe with a fresh edge on him, a few extra facets revealed. That was what mattered to me then. That I was still myself. You had to serve some master, be it employer, overlord, presdent, corporation, god. It was the way of the world. And I decided, as if I had a choice, that Montezuma couldn't screw it up worse than whatever god he was replacing. So long as I had the power to pretend to be myself—which is all people really have of themselves—I was fine with it.

"You know what's goin' on here?" Lupe asked me as we lay facing one another, so close the tips of her breasts grazed my chest.

"With this whole trip? I think I got a line on it."

She toyed with the ends of my hair. "It feels weird to love you. I mean, I always did, y'know…but it was like, Okay, I love him, but fuck it. I got stuff to do. And now"—she gave a shrug—"it feels weird."

"But it feels good, too," I said and pulled her closer.

"Yeah, it feels good." She sounded doubtful.

"What?" I said. "What's the matter?"

"We didn't have a lot to do with gettin' here," she said. "If we hadn't done the story on the Carbonells, maybe things woulda stayed the same."

"Hey," I said. "If my papa hadn't been such a screw-up, we never woulda met. If you were a guy, we wouldn't be havin' this conversation. That kinda shit's true anytime."

"I know, but…"

"What're we gonna do? We're stuck with it."

"I ain't stuck! I can do what the hell I want!"

"You think that's ever been true?" I asked.

She pushed herself away from me, folded her arms and looked up toward the flowing template. "You startin' to remind me of Zee…with all his everything-is-everything else bullshit." Then less than a minute later, as I caressed her shoulder, she came back into my arms, apologized and said she loved me. But I was glad to have learned that Lupe was still Lupe, still contrary and willful.

"Y'know what really bothers me?" she said. "It ain't about me lovin' you, it's wonderin' how come you love me...if that's just Montezuma doin' it."

"I been in love with you since I was kid," I told her. "Since I saw you in church in your white lace dress."

She pulled back and gave me a stern look. "That was all bullshit."

"That's who you wanted to be," I said. "So that's who you are."

She turned onto her side. "It's that easy, huh? We get to be who we want to be?"

"I saw you," I said. "I saw who you are. You never were the Border Rose. That was your hustle...it wasn't you."

"You saw me?"

"Yeah...didn't you see me? When the light got real bright?"

"Sure, I did." She grinned. "You're still a dick."

I grabbed her, wrestled her into submission. The contact restored my erection, and she said, "See?"

We made love again, and afterward I felt subdued, restless, ready for something new.

"What do we do now?" Lupe asked. "Can we get outa here?"

"Maybe we should find out," I said in answer to both questions.

●

Our clothes, as newly fresh as we were, lay beside the bed. We dressed and went to the edge of the marble floor and then, because it seemed the only logical way out of the kingdom, we stepped forward. Once again I experienced that strobing effect, that flashing in and out of consciousness. It wasn't as disorienting as before. But when our feet touched ground and my vision stabilized, I was startled to find that we were in the desert. The stars were out, and the moon high. Sand and rock glowed palely. The personnel carrier in which we had fled the Carbonells was directly ahead of us, and Dennard was leaning against the hood. Frankie, who had been perched on the fender, jumped down and began shooting us as we came up.

"This little son of a bitch makin' us famous," Dennard said, gesturing with his rifle at Frankie. "I was listenin' to the radio. Whole damn world been watchin' your show."

With his tattoos and muscles, he remained a scary-looking individual, but he seemed thoroughly relaxed and un-Sammylike. I wasn't sure what he was doing there.

"What's goin' on?" I asked him.

"Waitin' for you is all." He said this amiably, and waved at the hills behind the carrier. "Some of Ramiro's people followed us from the barrio. Took 'em a long time to find us. They didn't get here till an hour ago."

"Where are they?" Lupe asked.

"I dealt with 'em." Dennard straightened. "I put one in back 'case you wanted to see."

He led us around the side of the carrier and flung open the rear door. It took me a moment to recognize Felix Carbonell. Most of his hair had been burned off, and the skin of his face was bloody and blistered. His flat black eyes, shiny and full of crazy rage, gave him away. His clothing was foul, tattered, but he still had his gold rings and necklaces. When he recognized me, he let out a string of enfeebled curses. His spittle was bloody.

"Man's had a rough week," Dennard said.

Frankie scuttled into the carrier to get a close-up of Felix.

I was more interested in Dennard than Felix—he seemed much the same as he had been before visiting the kingdom. Just like me and Lupe. I recalled what Zee had said about him being the same as he was before he met his father, only purified. I was beginning to suspect that Zee had always been a religious nut. Montezuma had made him into an efficient nut—which might mean that the religious gloss on what was happening had been applied by Zee. What did that make me and Lupe? More efficient hustlers, I supposed.

"What you want to do with him?" asked Dennard, and Lupe said, "Leave his ass. Maybe Montezuma can use him."

Felix struggled as Dennard helped him from the carrier, but he was too far gone to cause any trouble. *"Puto maricon!"* he said. *"Chu cha!"*

The accord among Lupe, Dennard, and me struck me as peculiar. For three people who had recently been at odds, we were getting along extremely well. No apparent distrust or doubt. It seemed we had been together for years.

Dennard propped Felix against a boulder. I scanned the hilltops for riders. None were in sight, but I knew one would be popping up any time to sniff Felix out. He sat there dribbling blood and curses. If we saw him again, he'd be a lot more reasonable, but I doubted I'd ever warm up to the guy.

"El Rayo?" asked Dennard, wiping some of Felix's blood off on his fatigues.

"Where else?" I glanced at Lupe, who spread her hands in a gesture of bewilderment.

Dennard piled in the driver's side of the carrier, and Lupe sat between us. We didn't talk much on the drive to El Rayo. I assumed Lupe and Dennard were, like me, assessing themselves, trying to understand where we were going and why we were going together, and I was also wondering what this whole thing had been about. Had Montezuma actually been negotiating with the Carbonells, or had his real intent been serious media exposure, an announcement of his presence? Gods were given to that sort of big opening. Burning bushes, virgin births. All that lightning-bolt-from-Olympus crap. Montezuma's birth had been as virgin as they could come, and his blissfully mad prophet had been right in step with John the Baptist and the rest. You had to figure the Son would be along any moment. Maybe we had that to look forward to.

But unlike Zee, I had no certainty. Who could say if Montezuma was a machine chumping itself into playing god, or if this was how gods happened, or if god was just mindless process, an incarnation of principle working things out over and over until he got it right...and you knew he was never going to get it right. We drove past the stone head. In its glowing eyes were speeding images of the personnel carrier. Signs of our advent. Dennard switched on the radio, tuned in a border station. A call-in show. People were asking what was this deal about an eternity, this for-real paradise? They asked who was Dennard? Was he Sammy or what? They asked personal questions about Lupe and me. Were we truly in love, or was it just for the show? Was Frankie a puppet? We weren't just tabloid creatures now—we were celebrity heroes. The host talked about the party going on in the streets, celebrating the notion that God's kingdom might be real, and that El Rayo, this unimportant residue that had collected at the bottom of America, this thin red line of poverty and madness, might have a destiny to fulfill. Then he played an interview with Papa, who was his usual supportive self.

"My son is not unintelligent," he said, doing his professor delivery. "But he doesn't use his intellect. He mistakes bravado for true courage, and he's less competent than lucky. But he is *very* lucky. I think that what's happened proves my point."

"Asshole!" Lupe switched the radio off.

When we came to El Rayo, I needed a moment to pull it together. I told Dennard to stop on the outskirts, a weedy patch extending from the backs of two ruined houses, fragments of their whitewashed walls still erect. We climbed out, and Frankie scuttled off to get a wide shot of the three of us. Dennard took a stand, rifle at the ready. Lupe and I held hands and stared at El Rayo, at the fiery fence dividing the sky and the violent places beneath it, the sewer worshippers of Barrio Ningun and the cartels and the gangs, the dog men and the wasted women, the wretched and the insane, all the delirium and grief of that least of cities…

Our city.

Between buildings some 200 feet away, the lights of Calle 99 burned in crumbling gold bars. I heard a faint riotous music and joyful shrieks. Frankie must have been transmitting live because before long people started coming out from the backs of buildings and alleyways, realizing the picture they'd been watching was being shot close by. They kept their distance, probably worried about Dennard, but they shouted our names.

Lupe waved at them, our welcomers, and they shouted louder.

I felt a quickness of self I'd never before known. Some things were coming clear, the little glittering pieces fitting into place, the fragmented thoughts I'd had since entering the kingdom beginning to cohere into a structure. But I didn't need to think about any of it. Even if the future was pre-ordained, written in silicon, I was never going to understand what was happening. Not even god could understand it all. Everything was different, but everything was more-

or-less the same, and I'd had enough of the unfamiliar, the incomprehensible, the strange. I wanted to walk the streets of El Rayo, have a drink at Cruzados, join the party that was being thrown in our honor, and I gestured toward the lights, the music, the fire in the sky, and to Lupe who was looking at me happily, as if I were something she truly liked to see, I said, "Hey, what about it, girl? You'n me...a little fiesta? It ain't such a bad night to have no future."